PATRICK G

GHOST IN THE MACHINE

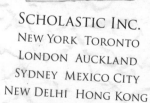

SCHOLASTIC INC.
NEW YORK TORONTO
LONDON AUCKLAND
SYDNEY MEXICO CITY
NEW DELHI HONG KONG

PC STUDIO

ISBN 978-0-545-28421-9

12 11 10 9 8 7 6 5 4 3 2 1   10 11 12 13 14 15/0

Printed in the U.S.A.   40

First Scholastic Book Clubs printing, September 2010

The text type was set in GFY Thornesmith.
Book design by Christopher Stengel
Illustrations by Joshua Pease

AM I REALLY DOING THIS?

WHAT'S TAKING HER SO LONG?

IT'S COLD IN HERE.

I CAN'T GO DOWN THERE AGAIN.

BIRDIE CARVED IN WOOD UNDER THE GEARS. WHY?

CAREFUL NOW.

YOU HAVE BEEN WARNED.

REMOVE THIS CRYPTIX AND SUFFER THE CONSEQUENCE.

WHEN CURIOSITY MEETS DEADLY EXPLOSIVE FORCE.

THAT SOUND AGAIN — NOT THE STEPS — SOMETHING ELSE.

SARAH'S EYES ARE BIG. SHE'S TERRIFIED.

I COULDN'T SEE IT.

I ONLY FELT IT.

DON'T MAKE ME COME LOOKING FOR YOU.

FRANCIS PALMER. JORDAN HOOKE. WILSON BOYLE.

HECTOR NEWTON. JOSEPH BUSH. DAD.

GLADYS. THE APOSTLE. DR. WATTS.

Sunday, September 19, 7:20 a.m.

How did I get back in my room?

The last thing I remember really clearly is standing at the top of the stairs in the dredge and looking down. After that, everything is fuzzy around the edges. Something about seeing my own bloodstain on those old floorboards sort of did me in.

So it was shock. That's it — I was in shock. My brain was smart enough to shut down. I was a zombie, more or less.

I sure looked like one on that video.

I can piece this together. Between the video and my notes from the dredge, I'm sure I can do this. Brand-new journal, brand-new memories. I'm glad I started with a blank slate. It's like a new lease on life. This is totally going to work.

I remember walking up the alley and there she was, standing in the headlights with her camera on. I didn't realize how much I missed seeing her until I shuffled up on my crutches like an idiot and gave her the lamest hug ever.

I REMEMBER GETTING IN HER CAR AND FEELING VERY NERVOUS AS WE LEFT THE ALLEY, LIKE I WAS GOING TO THROW UP. SARAH DIDN'T WANT BONNER DRIVING AROUND AND SEEING HER CAR AND MAYBE COMING AFTER US IN THE MIDDLE OF THE NIGHT, SO WE PARKED A LONG WAY FROM THE TRAILHEAD. THIS MADE THE ENDLESS WALK THROUGH THE WOODS SEEM EVEN LONGER. LET ME TELL YOU, DRAGGING A WRAPPED-UP LEG THROUGH THE WOODS IS NO PICNIC. IT'S A LONG HOOF OUT THERE — I MEAN REALLY LONG. BY THE TIME WE GOT THERE I WAS THINKING WE'D MADE A BIG MISTAKE.

I'M SURE THAT'S WHY I SCRIBBLED A-M I REALLY DOING THIS? AT THE TOP OF THE FIRST PAGE OF THIS NEW JOURNAL. (FOR OBVIOUS REASONS, I DIDN'T WANT TO TAKE THE OLD ONE WITH ME AND RISK IT BEING LOST OR, I DON'T KNOW, CAPTURED.) AND THOSE NEXT WORDS — WHAT'S TAKING HER SO LONG? — I REMEMBER THOSE WORDS, TOO. WE'D FINALLY ARRIVED AT THE DREDGE, AND SARAH LEFT ME ALONE WITH THE CAMERA. I PANNED IT OVER EACH OF THE WINDOWS IN THE DREDGE WHILE I WAITED FOR HER TO COME BACK AND TELL ME SHE'D CUT THE LOCK ON THE DOOR. I

DIDN'T WANT TO SEE A GHOST IN ONE OF THOSE WINDOWS, BUT I COULDN'T STOP LOOKING FOR ONE. WHEN SARAH CAME BACK, I FOLLOWED HER DOWN THE LAST PART OF THE PATH.

BEFORE I KNEW IT, WE WERE INSIDE.

IT'S COLD IN HERE.

I REMEMBER THINKING IT WAS CHILLY. SEPTEMBER IN SKELETON CREEK IS PRECEDED BY A LONG WARM SUMMER THAT LULLS YOU TO SLEEP. THEN BANG, THE COLD NIGHTS SHOW UP OUT OF NOWHERE LIKE A SCREEN DOOR IN YOUR FACE.

SO IT WAS COLD IN THE DREDGE, AND THAT'S WHY SARAH WAS TALKING WITH A TINY PATTERN OF STARTS AND STOPS IN HER VOICE. IT WASN'T BECAUSE SHE WAS AFRAID. SHE WAS COLD.

I CAN'T GO DOWN THERE AGAIN.

THIS IS WHERE THE SHOCK SET IN, I'M PRETTY SURE. I DIDN'T SAY I COULDN'T GO DOWN THE STAIRS AGAIN, BUT WHEN WE REACHED THE TOP, I KNEW I COULDN'T DO IT. STAIRS WERE A BAD OMEN IN EVERY ALFRED HITCHCOCK MOVIE I'D EVER SEEN, A PRELUDE TO SOMETHING SINISTER ABOUT TO HAPPEN. AND WHAT WAS MUCH WORSE, THIS WAS THE PLACE I'D HAD THE

ACCIDENT AND ALMOST DIED. THAT WAS IT FOR ME. IT WAS EITHER GET OUT BY ANOTHER WAY OR DIE TRYING. I REMEMBER HOW IT FELT TO BE BACK THERE, SORT OF LIKE SOMEONE HAD CUT OFF THE OXYGEN TO MY LUNGS AND LEFT ME FOR DEAD. I FLOATED THROUGH THE REST AND THEN I WOKE UP IN MY BED.

I STILL CAN'T BELIEVE EVERYTHING ON THAT VIDEO.

SOMEHOW MY ZOMBIE FORM ARRIVED INSIDE THE SECRET ROOM. SEEING THAT VIDEO REMINDED ME OF SOMETHING. I SAW THE BIRDIE CARVED IN WOOD. I REMEMBER LEANING OVER INTO THE GEARS INSTINCTIVELY AND GLANCING DOWN INTO THE OPENING. THERE'S A MEMORY PACKED IN FROZEN STORAGE SOMEWHERE IN WHICH I'VE DONE THIS BEFORE. I CAN'T CRACK THE ICE, BUT IT'S THERE.

WHAT JOLTED ME BACK TO REALITY? IT MUST HAVE BEEN SEEING SARAH TURNING THE DIALS AT THE SAME TIME I WAS READING THE WARNING ABOUT THE WHOLE PLACE EXPLODING. IT WAS LIKE SHE HAD A STICK OF LIT DYNAMITE IN HER HAND.

<u>STOP TOUCHING IT!</u>

I SCREAMED THESE WORDS, OR AT LEAST I THOUGHT I DID. BUT WATCHING THE VIDEO, I SEE THAT I ONLY

SCREAMED IN MY HEAD. I HATE THAT I CAN'T TRUST WHAT I SAW AND WHAT I FELT. IT'S LIKE A REPEAT OF THE NIGHT I FELL, WITH EVERYTHING GRAYED OUT. I STILL CAN'T REMEMBER THE RIGHT ORDER OR WHETHER CERTAIN THINGS HAPPENED OR NOT. THE SCARIEST THING ABOUT WATCHING SARAH'S VIDEOS IS THAT I DON'T ALWAYS KNOW WHAT'S COMING NEXT.

THAT SOUND AGAIN.

OKAY, THIS I RECALL PERFECTLY. I'VE READ THOSE THREE WORDS ON THE FIRST PAGE OF THIS JOURNAL FOUR OR FIVE TIMES ALREADY, AND EVERY TIME I HEAR THE SAME SOUNDS. IT'S LIKE A SOUNDTRACK. THAT SOUND AGAIN, THAT SOUND AGAIN, THAT SOUND AGAIN. I CAN'T DESCRIBE IT, BUT I HEARD IT AT LEAST TWICE IN THE VIDEO. ONCE WHEN WE WERE IN THE ALLEY AND ONCE WHEN I SAW THE BIRDIE. I NEED TO WATCH THAT VIDEO AGAIN BECAUSE I CAN'T SAY FOR SURE IF THE SOUND IS REALLY THERE OR NOT. IT'S LIKE I SEE THINGS — THE GHOST OR THE BIRDIE — AND I HEAR THE SOUND. AM I HEARING IT IN MY HEAD? IS THERE SOME SORT OF VISUAL CUE THAT'S MAKING MY BRAIN CREATE THE SOUND? OR IS THE SOUND REALLY THERE?

I SCRIBBLED THE NAMES. A-LL OF THEM. BUT HERE'S THE STRANGE PART: I DON'T REMEMBER WHEN I WROTE THE NAMES DOWN. IT'S AN AWFUL LOT TO REMEMBER, ALL THOSE NAMES, BUT I DON'T THINK I WROTE THEM UNTIL LATER. BELIEVE IT OR NOT, I THINK I WOKE UP IN THE DARK IN MY OWN BED AND DID IT. I'VE ACTUALLY DONE THIS BEFORE, WHEN I WAS SMALL. I USED TO DO IT ALL THE TIME. I'D WAKE UP WHEN I WAS FIVE OR SIX YEARS OLD AND FIND THAT I'D DRAWN THE WORDS GREEN EGZ HAM IN CRAYON ON THE WALL IN THE MIDDLE OF THE NIGHT.

"WHY DID YOU DO THAT?" MY DAD WOULD ASK IN THE MORNING.

"I WAS ASLEEP. SOMEONE ELSE DID IT."

"WE'VE TOLD YOU NOT TO WRITE ON YOUR WALLS," DAD WOULD SAY, ALL STERN LIKE HE WAS GOING TO PUNISH ME.

"I DIDN'T DO IT," I'D INSIST.

"IS THAT SO? THEN WHO DID?"

"DID YOU LOCK THE DOORS LAST NIGHT?"

MY DAD (AND MY MOM, FOR THAT MATTER) KNEW THEN WHAT THEY KNOW NOW: I COULD TALK THEM INTO

THEIR GRAVES IF THEY LET ME. I COULD GO ON AND ON ABOUT WHETHER THEY LOCKED THE WINDOWS AND CHECKED EVERY ROOM AND FLUSHED THE TOILETS AND A HUNDRED OTHER THINGS THAT MIGHT OR MIGHT NOT HAVE TO DO WITH HOW MY WALLS GOT COVERED IN PURPLE CRAYON.

"STOP WRITING ON YOUR WALLS."

THAT'S ALL MY DAD HAD THE ENERGY TO SAY ONCE HE COULD SEE I WAS HEADING DOWN A PATH THAT MIGHT TAKE TWENTY MINUTES AND WOULD LEAD ABSOLUTELY NOWHERE.

MOST OF THE TIME, OR SO IT SEEMS TO ME, IF DAD SAYS ANYTHING IN MY GENERAL DIRECTION, IT'S EITHER A WARNING OR A REPRIMAND. I HAVE COME TO ACCEPT THIS FACT, WHICH TECHNICALLY SPEAKING IS PRETTY SAD.

AT LEAST HE NEVER YELLS AT ME.

SO ANYWAY, THIS IDEA OF SLEEPWRITING LIKE SOMEONE MIGHT SLEEPWALK, I THINK IT MIGHT HAVE REVISITED ME LAST NIGHT. BECAUSE I'M JUST ABOUT SURE I DIDN'T CONSCIOUSLY WRITE THOSE NAMES ON THE FRONT PAGE. LOOKING AT THE SCRAWLED NAMES, I'M

ASKING MYSELF, JUST LIKE MY DAD USED TO ASK: WHY DID YOU DO THAT?

FRANCIS PALMER. JORDAN HOOKE. WILSON BOYLE. DR. WATTS. WHO ARE THESE PEOPLE? AND WHAT ABOUT HECTOR NEWTON AND THE APOSTLE — WHO ARE THEY? I'VE NEVER HEARD OF A SINGLE ONE OF THEM, SO WHY ARE THEIR NAMES CARVED IN STONE INSIDE A SECRET ROOM ON THE DREDGE?

AND WHILE WE'RE AT IT, WHY IS MY DAD'S NAME HIDDEN IN THAT ROOM RIGHT UNDER JOE BUSH'S NAME? AND THE LOCAL LIBRARIAN?

SARAH'S EYES ARE BIG. SHE'S TERRIFIED.

I COULDN'T SEE IT.

I ONLY FELT IT.

I'M GLAD I DIDN'T SEE OLD JOE BUSH FOR MYSELF WHEN WE WERE TRAPPED IN THE SECRET ROOM. I'M GLAD I WAS WEDGED IN THERE, FACING THE WALL SO I COULDN'T TURN AROUND. SEEING A GHOST ON VIDEO IS BAD ENOUGH; I DON'T NEED TO SEE IT IN PERSON.

LATER IN THE CAR — I SORT OF REMEMBER THIS CONVERSATION NOW — SARAH SAID IT WAS THE SCARIEST THING SHE'D EVER SEEN, LIKE WHATEVER

TERRIBLE THING WAS OUT THERE HAD HER TRAPPED AND WANTED HER DEAD. SHE SAID THE GHOST OF OLD JOE BUSH SNIFFED THE AIR, WHICH I DIDN'T REALLY GET FROM WATCHING THE VIDEO, BUT THAT'S HOW SHE FELT ABOUT IT. WHEN HE LEANED IN, SHE SAW HIS FACE AND ALMOST SCREAMED. SHE'D WANTED TO SCREAM, BUT OLD JOE BUSH WAS ALMOST TOUCHING THE BACK OF MY HEAD AND SHE WAS COMPLETELY PARALYZED WITH FEAR.

I REMEMBER SOMETHING ELSE NOW, SOMETHING HORRIBLE. I REMEMBER AT THAT MOMENT IT FELT EXTRA COLD, LIKE A GIANT BLOCK OF ICE WAS ABOUT TO TOUCH THE BACK OF MY NECK.

BUT I DIDN'T TURN AROUND. I DIDN'T GET TO SEE IT UNTIL I WATCHED THE VIDEO A FEW MINUTES AGO. THE MORE I REMEMBER, THE MORE I WISH SARAH HAD NEVER SHOWN IT TO ME.

THERE'S A BIG GAP NOW, A WHOLE SECTION I JUST DON'T REMEMBER AT ALL. I DON'T REMEMBER GETTING OUT OF THE SECRET ROOM OR COMING TO THE STAIRS AND INSISTING ONCE AGAIN THAT I COULDN'T GO DOWN. I DON'T REMEMBER RACING THROUGH PARTS OF THE

DREDGE I'D NEVER SEEN BEFORE OR COWERING IN THE CORNER. I ABSOLUTELY DON'T RECALL GETTING BACK UP AND MAKING MYSELF HOBBLE FORWARD UNTIL WE CAME TO THE WAY OUT.

<u>DON'T MAKE ME COME LOOKING FOR YOU.</u>

A MESSAGE SMEARED ON THE DOOR. THE KIND OF WORDS THAT SAY <u>DON'T YOU DARE TELL THE COPS, DON'T TELL YOUR PARENTS, DON'T TRUST ANYONE IN THIS TOWN, AND, MOST OF ALL, DON'T EVER COME BACK INTO THE DREDGE AGAIN.</u>

<u>THAT</u> I REMEMBER. I REMEMBER IT MORE THAN ANYTHING ELSE FROM LAST NIGHT, FOR THE WORST POSSIBLE REASON. I REMEMBER IT BECAUSE WHEN I WOKE UP THIS MORNING, I GOT OUT OF BED AND SHUFFLED OVER TO MY DESK. WHEN I TURNED AROUND, I SAW THAT I'D SCRAWLED THOSE VERY WORDS ON THE WALL OVER MY BED.

IT'S VERY DISTURBING WHEN YOU COME TO THE REALIZATION THAT YOU'VE BEEN AWAKE WITHOUT KNOWING IT, DOING BIZARRE THINGS YOU CAN'T RECALL.

THEN AGAIN, MAYBE I DIDN'T WRITE THE MESSAGE ON THE WALL OVER MY BED.

It could be someone else's writing.

I guess it could be my dad's or Ranger Bonner's.

Or, more likely, the ghost of Old Joe Bush followed me home so he could make sure I understood him the first time.

Sunday, September 19, 8:15 a.m.

I just spent the last twenty minutes standing on my bed with a wet rag, scrubbing words off the wall. Ink is a lot harder to wash off than a purple crayon. It's especially difficult because my leg is still killing me and standing on my bed without falling off is a real trick.

For some reason the word <u>Don't</u> was darker than all the other words, so it reads more like <u>Don't make me come looking for you</u>. But it didn't really matter, because twenty minutes of scrubbing did almost nothing to remove the words. What I really need is some sandpaper and a can of paint.

I moved my <u>Dark Side of the Moon</u> poster to cover the message. I haven't even noticed that poster for months and months — I think I only ever listened to Pink Floyd for about a week in the eighth grade to begin with. I have no idea why I still have it hanging in my room.

My mom came in a few minutes later and stood over my bed, staring at the poster I'd moved.

"I used to listen to that music when I was your age," she said. "Did I ever tell you that?"

She'd told me about a thousand times, so I nodded.

"Why did you move it?"

I shrugged and changed subjects, hoping she wouldn't notice I'd pinned it up slightly crooked and try to fix it.

"I think I'll stay in bed a little longer. I didn't sleep so well last night."

Mom was still staring at the poster, like it brought back some memory she hadn't had in a while. Then she looked down at me.

"Your dad wants you out of this room and doing something with your life. Back to school in only a week, remember? You've really got to get used to walking on that leg."

If only she'd known how far out of my room I'd been the night before. I gave her my tired look, which wasn't hard because I was exhausted.

She sighed. "I can hold him off another half hour with bacon and eggs." Then she went to the

DOOR AND TURNED BACK FOR ONE MORE LOOK AT THE POSTER. "YOU KNOW IT'S CROOKED, RIGHT?"

I CLOSED MY EYES LIKE I WAS DOZING OFF AND NEARLY FELL ASLEEP BY ACCIDENT.

WHEN THE DOOR WAS SHUT AND I WAS SURE SHE WAS GONE, I PULLED MY PHONE OUT FROM UNDER MY PILLOW. SARAH HAD SAID 8:30 A.M. AND IT WAS 8:30 A.M. THERE WAS A ONE-WORD TEXT MESSAGE ON MY SCREEN, WHICH I RECOGNIZED FROM ONE OF MY FAVORITE BOOKS. DOES SARAH THINK I'M LOSING MY GRIP ON REALITY, JUST LIKE JACK TORRANCE DID? I WISH I COULD REMEMBER EVERYTHING FROM LAST NIGHT, BUT I CAN'T. MAYBE I AM GOING CRAZY AND I JUST DON'T KNOW IT. I SUPPOSE IF I WERE LOSING MY MARBLES, I'D BE THE LAST ONE TO KNOW.

I DELETED THE PASSWORD, WENT TO MY DESK, AND LOGGED ON TO SARAH'S SITE.

SARAHFINCHER.COM
PASSWORD:
JACKTORRANCE

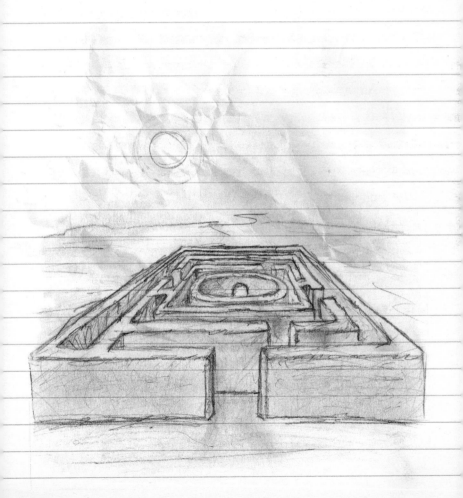

Sunday, September 19, 11:00 a.m.

I couldn't go back to sleep after watching Sarah's newest video . . . and I was hungry besides. The breakfast smell working its way up the stairs and under my door is tough to ignore, especially on Sunday morning when we actually get a weekly paper and Mom doesn't give me a hard time about drinking coffee. Any other morning she's on my case, but Sunday is a free pass for reasons I don't entirely understand.

Have you ever looked across the table, past a plate of scrambled eggs, bacon, and toast, and wondered if you could trust your own parents?

I just did.

"Where's Henry?" I said, and then I shoved most of a piece of toast in my mouth and washed it down with coffee. Henry is my dad's best friend, who visits from New York for a couple of weeks every year. He's got a complicated past when it comes to the dredge.

"Fishing," Dad said. He was staring at the paper, which was on the table next to his plate. He glanced up at me, then back at the editorial

PAGE. "You're going to school next week," he went on.

"I know."

"That's not a license to talk with Sarah Fincher. You know that, right?"

I didn't answer him. Inside I was seething, but there was no point saying anything. I was already talking with Sarah practically every day without either of my parents knowing about it. Getting their permission had found its way to the bottom of my priority list.

Mom piped in. "He knows, Paul. Just read your paper and let the boy eat in peace."

"All right, all right. But we agreed. School next week, no excuses. And no Sarah Fincher."

They blamed Sarah for my accident. They said she was trouble.

They were totally wrong about the first part.

The second part remained to be seen.

I finished my breakfast and came back to my room. I could tell Dad wanted to insist I go outside, but Mom was pretty mad about how he

19

WAS BADGERING ME, SO HE LEFT ME ALONE. I THINK I'VE
GOT A FEW HOURS OF PEACE AND QUIET UP HERE, AT
LEAST UNTIL HENRY GETS BACK. AFTER THAT, ALL
BETS ARE OFF. HE'LL WANT TO PLAY CARDS OR TALK.

WHAT'S MY DAD HIDING? HIS NAME IS ON A SLAB IN
THE DREDGE THAT TIES HIM TO A WHOLE BUNCH OF
OTHER NAMES. HE'S PART OF A SECRET SOCIETY. HE'S
GOT THE ALCHEMY SYMBOL FOR GOLD TATTOOED ON
HIS SHOULDER AND THAT ALCHEMIST DIAGRAM IN HIS
DRAWER.

IT HAS TO ADD UP TO SOMETHING. BUT WHAT?

I'LL START WITH THE NAMES FROM THE SECRET
ROOM — THAT'S MY BEST CLUE. I'LL WORK MY
WAY DOWN THE LIST AND FIGURE OUT WHO THESE
PEOPLE ARE.

MAYBE SOME OF THEM ARE STILL ALIVE.

LIKE THE LIBRARIAN.

LIKE MY FATHER.

OTHER THAN MY MOM STOPPING BY AN HOUR AGO WITH LUNCH, I'VE HAD THREE HOURS OF UNINTERRUPTED RESEARCH TIME ON MY LAPTOP. I KEEP IT VERY QUIET IN MY ROOM — NO MUSIC OR ANYTHING LIKE THAT — SO I COULD HEAR THE TING OF A BUTTER KNIFE ON THE EDGE OF A GLASS MAYONNAISE JAR AS SHE MADE MY SANDWICH. THIS WAS MY SIGNAL TO ERASE EVERYTHING I WAS WORKING ON. I'VE GOTTEN TO WHERE I CAN DO THIS AND RE-ENABLE THE SOFTWARE MY PARENTS THINK IS KEEPING TABS ON ME IN LESS THAN THIRTY SECONDS. UNLESS THEY'RE WATCHING WITH A CAMERA, THERE'S NO WAY THEY'RE KEEPING TRACK OF WHAT I'M DOING UP HERE.

I ALMOST SPILLED THE BEANS TO MY MOM WHEN SHE WAS IN HERE. IT'S LIKE I WANT TO TRUST HER, BUT SHE'S MARRIED TO MY DAD AND HE'S TANGLED UP IN THIS SECRET STUFF. SHE'D TELL HIM. I KNOW SHE WOULD. AND SHE WAS JUST AS MAD AT ME AFTER THE ACCIDENT. MAYBE MADDER.

AFTER MOM SET THE COKE AND THE SANDWICH ON MY DESK, SHE STARED OUT THE WINDOW.

"YOU COMING DOWN ANYTIME SOON?"

I SHRUGGED AND POPPED THE TOP ON THE COKE CAN.

"IS HENRY BACK YET?" I ASKED.

MY MOM SHOOK HER HEAD. "YOUR DAD WENT AFTER HIM. FISHING MUST BE GOOD."

I HESITATED A SECOND, THEN SAID, "HAVE YOU EVER BEEN IN THE OLD DREDGE, MOM?"

SHE LOOKED AT ME LIKE I WAS SLIPPING THROUGH HER FINGERS AND FALLING DOWN A STEEP HILL. YOU KNOW THE LOOK. THE ONE WHERE YOUR MOM THINKS YOU'RE IN TROUBLE BUT CAN'T HELP YOU.

"I HAVEN'T BEEN OUT TO THE DREDGE IN YEARS. WHY DO YOU ASK?"

I COULD SEE SHE WAS NERVOUS, LIKE I WAS DANCING AROUND THE EDGE OF SOMETHING SHE WAS AFRAID TO HEAR. SO I TOTALLY BACKED OFF.

"NO REASON. IT'S BEEN OUT THERE A LONG TIME. I FIGURED YOU'D BEEN INSIDE."

SHE LOOKED RELIEVED, WHICH MADE ME GLAD I HADN'T TOLD HER I WAS SEEING GHOSTS, HANGING OUT WITH SARAH, AND WANDERING AROUND THE DREDGE IN THE MIDDLE OF THE NIGHT GETTING TRAPPED IN SECRET ROOMS. MY MOM WANTED A NORMAL SON, WHO WAS IN

SCHOOL AND DIDN'T GET INTO STRANGE KINDS OF TROUBLE ALL THE TIME. I CAN'T REALLY SAY THAT I BLAME HER.

"EAT YOUR SANDWICH," SHE SAID, AND THEN WE TALKED ABOUT SOMETHING ELSE. (IT'LL MAKE MORE SENSE IF I EXPLAIN IT LATER. BUT WE DID TALK SOME MORE.)

THEN SHE LEFT AND I WAS ALL ALONE.

THAT WAS THE ONLY INTERRUPTION I HAD IN A VERY SUCCESSFUL THREE HOURS ONLINE, AS DETECTIVE WORK GOES.

HERE'S WHAT I DID:

FIRST I MADE A LIST OF ALL THE NAMES THAT WERE ON THE SLAB IN THE SECRET ROOM. I ADDED DARYL BONNER'S NAME TO THE LIST BECAUSE I DON'T TRUST HIM AT ALL. NEITHER DOES SARAH. THE NAMES BECAME, I GUESS, MY SUSPECT LIST. SUSPECTS OF WHAT CRIME, I DON'T KNOW — YET.

BUT I'M CLOSER TO FINDING SOME ANSWERS NOW THAN I WAS LAST NIGHT.

THIS WAS THE LIST I BEGAN WITH, IN THE ORDER I WANTED TO INVESTIGATE THEM:

JOSEPH BUSH

FRANCIS PALMER

PAUL MCCRAY

Gladys Morgan

The Apostle

Dr. Watts

Jordan Hooke

Wilson Boyle

Hector Newton

Daryl Bonner

First things first: Scratch Joseph Bush from the list.

That guy is already dead.

I went back to my old journal and read my entry from September 13th. I've torn it out and moved it here as evidence:

The greatest discovery — or the worst, depending on how you look at it — that Sarah and I made involved the untimely death of a workman on the dredge. There was only one mention of the incident in the newspaper, and nothing anywhere else. Old Joe Bush is what they called him, so I can only conclude that he was not a young man. Old Joe Bush had let his pant leg get caught in the gears, and the

MACHINERY OF THE DREDGE HAD PULLED HIM THROUGH, CRUSHING HIS LEG BONE INTO GRAVEL. THEN THE DREDGE SPIT HIM OUT INTO THE GRIMY WATER. HIS LEG WAS DEMOLISHED, AND UNDER THE DEAFENING SOUND IN THE DARK NIGHT, NO ONE HEARD HIM SCREAM.

OLD JOE BUSH NEVER EMERGED FROM THE BLACK POND BELOW.

WHENEVER I SEE OR HEAR THAT NAME, MY LEG STARTS TO ACHE AND I THINK OF ALL THE TIMES I'VE SEEN AND HEARD WHAT REMAINS OF OLD JOE BUSH. I'VE HEARD HIM WITH MY OWN EARS, DRAGGING THAT CRUSHED LEG ACROSS THE OLD FLOOR OF THE DREDGE. I'VE SEEN FOOTAGE OF HIM — AM I REALLY SAYING THIS? — SEEN HIM THROUGH THE BROKEN WINDOW AND LEANING DOWN INTO THE SECRET ROOM AND MOVING ACROSS A CAMERA THAT'S BEEN DROPPED. I'VE FELT HIM PUSH ME OVER A RAIL, HIGH ENOUGH OFF THE GROUND TO KILL ME.

THE IMPORTANT THING RIGHT NOW IS THAT JOSEPH BUSH IS OFF THE LIST. AND HE'S NOT THE ONLY

WORKER WHO DIED ON THE DREDGE. I SEARCHED AND
SEARCHED FOR FRANCIS PALMER AND DIDN'T HAVE ANY
LUCK AT ALL UNTIL I REMEMBERED ALL THOSE MINUTES
AND REPORTS FROM THE NEW YORK GOLD AND
SILVER COMPANY. THOSE WERE BIG FILES AND THERE
WERE LOTS OF THEM, PLUS I HAD GONE IN AND STARTED
HIGHLIGHTING DIFFERENT AREAS OF INTEREST. I COULDN'T
KEEP THOSE FILES ON MY COMPUTER, SO I'D
TRANSFERRED THEM TO A FLASH DRIVE AND TAPED IT
UNDER ONE OF THE DRAWERS TO MY DESK.

AND YOU KNOW WHAT? IT'S A GOOD THING I DID
THAT. BECAUSE WHEN I WENT LOOKING FOR THOSE FILES
ONLINE A COUPLE OF HOURS AGO, A BIG CHUNK OF THEM
WERE GONE. SOMEONE, SOMEWHERE, WAS ABLE TO
CLASSIFY THOSE OLD FILES OR KNEW SOMEONE WAS
LOOKING AT THEM. MAYBE THEY TRACKED MY IP
ADDRESS TO SKELETON CREEK AND DIDN'T LIKE
SOMEONE SNOOPING AROUND. IT'S NOT A GOOD SIGN
THAT THINGS FROM THE PAST ARE BEING HIDDEN AWAY.
PEOPLE ONLY HIDE REPORTS IF THEY THINK SOMEONE
WILL FIND SOMETHING BAD IN THEM.

WHICH IS EXACTLY WHAT I FOUND.

I PULLED UP THE FILES FROM THAT FLASH DRIVE AND RAN A PROGRAM I HAVE THAT WILL SIFT THROUGH MULTIPLE DOCUMENTS FOR KEY WORDS ALL AT ONE TIME. I PUT IN THE KEY WORDS <u>FRANCIS PALMER</u>. I GOT A RETURN ON A DOCUMENT DATED WITHIN MONTHS OF THE DEATH OF JOSEPH BUSH. WHEN I HIGHLIGHTED THE ENTRY FROM A BOARD OF DIRECTORS MEETING, I REALIZED THE DEATH OF FRANCIS PALMER TOOK PLACE ONLY TWENTY-SEVEN DAYS AFTER THE DEATH OF JOSEPH BUSH.

NYGS PM Mins. -- Paragraph 9, page 25.

The #42 asset holding in Skeleton Creek, Oregon, was the location of a fatal accident on 8-12-63. The second fatality in less than a month has led to an internal safety and structural investigation of assets #31-#47. The victim, Francis Palmer, was a long-term night shift control room operator. He was found dead in the water below asset #42, an apparent accidental drowning. Legal department advises adding safety precautions to asset #42 in the form of railings and window bars. Approved. Cost analysis for modifications to asset #42 scheduled for 9-15. Insurance claims pending with Palmer family.

SCRATCH FRANCIS PALMER OFF THE LIST.

DEAD.

HE AND JOE BUSH WERE BOTH IN THE CROSSBONES AND BOTH OF THEM DIED ON THE DREDGE WITHIN A MONTH OF EACH OTHER. I HAD A BRIEF MOMENT OF CONCERN AS MY DAD'S FACE FLASHED BEFORE MY EYES. TWENTY PERCENT OF THE PEOPLE ON THE LIST HAD ALREADY BEEN KILLED OFF, AND I HADN'T EVEN BEEN INVESTIGATING FOR AN HOUR.

THE NEXT TWO PEOPLE ON THE LIST WERE DAD AND GLADYS MORGAN, THE LIBRARIAN. I AT LEAST KNOW THESE TWO ARE STILL ALIVE. FOR SOME REASON

I just couldn't go searching around online for my dad. It was too weird. Who knew what kind of junk I might dig up about Paul McCray? He was involved, he was alive, he was secretive like everyone else in town, he'd lived here his whole life, he had a diagram with symbols and strange statements on it, he had a secret tattoo, and he was living in the same house as me.

So I moved on to Gladys Morgan, expecting to find out she was a dreary old windbag with a long, eventless life full of long, eventless days, weeks, and months.

Boy, was I wrong.

The first thing I found? Gladys Morgan hasn't always stayed in Skeleton Creek, contrary to what she tells everyone. She also spent some time in New York City, if you can believe that. How do I know Gladys Morgan was in New York City? Because the <u>New York Times</u> is archived online, and Gladys Morgan once made the news. That's right — <u>our</u> Gladys Morgan — in the <u>New York Times</u>! And here's

THE MOST INTERESTING PART: SHE WAS IN THE NEWS RIGHT AFTER THE ACCIDENTS ON THE DREDGE OCCURRED.

HERE'S A SMALL PART OF THE ARTICLE I FOUND:

PROTEST ERUPTS OVER ENVIRONMENTAL ALLEGATIONS

New York Gold and Silver board members arrived on Park Avenue this morning and found more than fifty protesters from all across America. The company, which operates dozens of gold dredges in remote parts of Alaska, Oregon, and Montana, has come under fire in recent months for what many are calling a disregard for environmental concerns in small towns across the West.

One of those in attendance, Gladys Morgan, came all the way from rural Oregon to join in the protest.

"They've got some explaining to do, simple as that," Morgan said. She, like many of those in attendance, lives in a small town where a New York Gold and Silver dredge grinds along the outskirts of town twenty-four hours a day, seven days a week. "They haven't kept up their end of the bargain. I'm here to tell them they're gonna, whether they like it or not."

Jim Pearson, a lumber mill worker from Billings, Montana, who drove the entire 3,000-mile journey with his dog, Skipper, had similar complaints.

What was she doing there? I get that she was angry, but going all the way to New York to complain with a bunch of other small-town folks? I think there was more to it than that. What if she was there as a member of the Crossbones? Two of them were dead in the span of a month. Or maybe the whole thing was a cover, especially her participation in this rally, and she worked for New York Gold and Silver all along. She could have killed them both. It's possible. She sure has the temper for it.

In detective terms, I think the evidence clearly points to Gladys Morgan as a person of interest.

The next name on my list, The Apostle, led nowhere. I couldn't find anything online that made any sense or connected anyone with that title to Skeleton Creek or the dredge. The only thing I can think of now is to check with one of the old churches in town. Maybe they know something. With a name like The Apostle, a house of worship seems like the most obvious place to look.

DR. WATTS — NOW THAT ONE'S INTERESTING. HE WAS SURPRISINGLY EASY TO FIND IN THE SKELETON CREEK HISTORICAL ARCHIVES. I WAS RIGHT IN THE MIDDLE OF WORKING ON THIS LEAD WHEN I HEARD MY MOM MAKING THE SANDWICH DOWNSTAIRS. THAT'S WHY, WHEN I WENT DOWN THERE, I STEERED THE CONVERSATION TO DR. WATTS, BECAUSE I FIGURED SHE WOULD HAVE HEARD OF HIM. WHEN I MENTIONED HIS NAME, SHE CRINGED.

"THAT OLD GEEZER?" SHE SAID. "HE HAD THE WORST BEDSIDE MANNER OF ANY DOCTOR I'VE EVER MET. AND HE HATED KIDS. I KNOW, BECAUSE I WAS ONE OF HIS PATIENTS."

"IS HE STILL ALIVE?" I ASKED.

"FAR AS I KNOW. I GUESS HE RETIRED ABOUT TWENTY YEARS AGO, BEFORE YOU WERE BORN. HE'D BE ABOUT EIGHTY BY NOW. HE'S RECLUSIVE. BUT HE LIVES RIGHT OFF MAIN STREET."

"YOU MEAN HE DOESN'T GET OUT MUCH?"

"I MEAN HE NEVER GETS OUT. AT LEAST I HAVEN'T SEEN HIM. MARY OVER AT THE STORE DELIVERS HIS GROCERIES AND CLEANS UP AFTER HIM. SHE SAYS HE'S OBSESSED WITH ALCHEMY. YOU KNOW WHAT THAT IS?"

I shook my head, not wanting her to know how much or how little I knew. The fact that Dr. Watts was into alchemy was a big deal.

"Well, it's sure not good medicine. Something about mixing metals or chemicals. I think it's making him soft in the head, whatever it is."

Very interesting. Dr. Watts is alive, so that makes three. And, just as important, he's messing around with alchemy, which has to be connected to the alchemy chart I found in my dad's dresser.

And speaking of threes — the last three names on the list inside the dredge were connected. Here's how I figured it out:

First I searched each of the names separately: Jordan Hooke, Wilson Boyle, Hector Newton. The searches for those names didn't lead anywhere interesting. Then I put all three names in at one time and searched them together. To my surprise, things started adding up. It was only the last names that mattered, and it quickly became clear that the first names were bogus, placed there to throw an outside observer off the track. Jordan, Wilson, and

Hector were there for show, but Hooke, Boyle, and Newton? Those were incredibly interesting last names when taken together.

Sir Isaac Newton — obviously I'd heard of him. Gravity and all. But the other two — both with the first name Robert — were even more interesting. Robert Hooke and Robert Boyle were contemporaries of Newton's and often worked right alongside him (if not in his enormous shadow). All three scientists were fiercely competitive and laid claim to similar finds.

Here's where the dots start to connect: Boyle in particular was a great enthusiast of alchemy. It was a secret fascination. As I read more about it, I began to understand that alchemy is, at least in part, the science of trying to turn one kind of metal into another. Boyle — I almost fell out of my chair when I read this — was totally obsessed with the properties of one thing in particular: gold.

Alchemy, gold, the dredge, the Crossbones, Dr. Watts — these things are all connected somehow. And that chart in my dad's dresser

34

DRAWER, THE ALCHEMIST DIAGRAM OF 79 FOR PAUL McCRAY.

HENRY AND MY DAD ARE GOING TO BE HOME SOON. I SHOULD GO DOWNSTAIRS AND SIT ON THE PORCH SO THEY DON'T WONDER WHAT I'M DOING UP HERE. NO SENSE GETTING THEM SUSPICIOUS WHEN I DON'T HAVE TO.

THIS IS WHAT I HAVE SO FAR:

~~JOSEPH BUSH~~ — DEAD

~~FRANCIS PALMER~~ — DEAD

PAUL McCRAY — MY DAD, ALCHEMY CHART

GLADYS MORGAN — NEW YORK VISIT

THE APOSTLE — SEND SARAH TO CHECK THE CHURCHES

DR. WATTS — ALIVE, ALCHEMY, RECLUSIVE

~~JORDAN HOOKE~~ — FABRICATED

~~WILSON BOYLE~~ — FABRICATED

~~HECTOR NEWTON~~ — FABRICATED

DARYL BONNER — SHOWS UP MYSTERIOUSLY, CAN'T BE TRUSTED

A FEW HOURS' WORK AND I'VE CUT THE LIST IN HALF.

NOT BAD.

SUNDAY, SEPTEMBER 19, 10:00 P.M.

It's clear my parents are serious about keeping me out of my room. And they've enlisted Henry to help them.

Is it really ten?

I'm tired.

As soon as I got out on the porch, Henry and my dad came back home. They'd caught a slew of fish (September is always good up here on the creek) and they didn't let up for almost an hour talking about this fly pattern and that rising fish and the one that got away. This is a little bit like watching a golf tournament on television, more background noise than anything that requires serious concentration.

About a half hour into this endless stream of fish talk, my mom informed me that Randy and Dennis were coming over for HBs with their parents. This was not good news. Randy and Dennis are brothers who live in town. My mom keeps trying to set us up, sort of like a playdate for teenagers.

36

These guys are about as interesting as dirt. We have exactly zero things in common, plus they're loud and they like to beat up on each other. I'm not even saying they're bad people, exactly — just that I can't think of a single reason why I would want to spend my Sunday evening listening to them talk about video games, dirt bikes, and farts.

But they showed up anyway because I couldn't bring myself to tell Mom to cancel and, truthfully, it was almost worth it for the HB.

An HB, in case I die and this journal is found in a ditch somewhere a hundred years from now, is a Henry Bomb. This is a burger that is huge beyond all reason. Part of the fun of having an HB is to see how much of it you can eat. No one, to my knowledge, has ever finished a Henry Bomb. My mom and Randy and Dennis's mom split HALF of one HB, if that tells you anything. And my mom is no slouch. She can put away a Whopper no problem. But this thing? Half an HB is like a whole meat loaf.

Our grill is pretty good size, but Henry only cooks one Henry Bomb at a time because they're extraordinarily "made to order." Tomatoes, lettuce, onions, special sauce (it's a secret, it's orange, and it's awesome), every kind of pepper, about a dozen ziplock bags filled with seasoning salt of varying degrees of heat (total wimp all the way up to blow your head off). Don't even get me started on the HB buns, which Henry makes himself from frozen bread dough (think Frisbee and you're in the ballpark).

I tried and failed to eat an entire HB.

It took a long time.

Just checked my phone and Sarah texted me:

9 EMV at 630am. MU EL

Delete.

Nine means her parents are watching. They must be paying closer attention than usual. Emailing Video at 6:30 a.m., she misses me, ends with Evil Laugh.

Actually, I'm sort of glad she's not sending me a video until tomorrow morning. Half the

TIME I GET THESE THINGS AT NIGHT AND THEN I CAN'T
SLEEP.

I'M TAKING FIVE MINUTES TO WRITE HER AN UPDATE
ON ALCHEMY AND THE APOSTLE AND EVERYTHING
ELSE I FIGURED OUT, AND THEN IT'S LIGHTS OUT.

MONDAY MORNING. EXACTLY ONE WEEK FROM NOW
I'LL BE GETTING READY FOR SCHOOL. MAYBE CLASSES
AND HOMEWORK WILL MAKE MY LIFE FEEL NORMAL
AGAIN.

THE SECOND I WOKE UP, I SAT UP AND LOOKED AT
ALL THE WALLS IN MY ROOM. THERE WAS NO NEW
WRITING. EITHER I COULDN'T FIND A PEN IN MY SLEEP
LAST NIGHT (THIS IS POSSIBLE SINCE I MADE A POINT OF
PUTTING EVERY PEN I HAVE AT THE BACK OF A DRAWER
AND SHUTTING IT TIGHT) OR WHOEVER WROTE THE FIRST
MESSAGE DOESN'T FEEL LIKE HE NEEDED TO TELL ME
TWICE.

AND THEN THERE WAS THIS OTHER, WORSE FEELING
AS I WOKE UP AND LOOKED AT THE POSTER I MOVED. IF
I LIFTED IT AND LOOKED UNDERNEATH, WOULD THE
WORDS EVEN BE THERE?

Don't Make Me Come Looking For You

THIS IS HOW MESSED UP MY MEMORY IS BECOMING.

CAN I EVEN TELL THE DIFFERENCE BETWEEN TRUTH
AND FICTION?

I CHECKED MY PHONE — NO PASSWORD. I CHECKED
MY EMAIL — NO PASSWORD. THEN I LOOKED OUT THE

WINDOW AND SAW A PIECE OF PAPER WAS TAPED TO THE OUTSIDE.

THIS CAN'T BE GOOD.

I PULLED THE WINDOW UP JUST FAR ENOUGH TO REACH MY HAND UNDER AND TAKE THE NOTE.

I COULD HEAR MY PARENTS TALKING DOWN THE HALL, GETTING READY TO LEAVE FOR WORK. HENRY WOULD SLEEP IN LATE AND PROBABLY GO FISHING. PRETTY SOON I'D HAVE THE HOUSE TO MYSELF.

HERE'S WHAT THE NOTE SAID:

No more email or text messaging for a couple days! My parents are really cracking down. Bonner stopped by here yesterday — Sunday, can you believe that? He told my parents someone had cut the lock on the dredge and gone back in. He came right out and said he suspected it was me. Unbelievable. He kept giving me the evil eye, like when I was in his office the other day. It's a good thing I grabbed those bolt cutters on the way out or we'd be finished. Don't be surprised if he shows up at your front door.

I got your message about the alchemy — veeeeery interesting. I wish we could sit down and talk! It's killing me. I'll do some digging at the church on the edge of town after school. For now, I've got some big news of my own — just go to the site and use castleofotranto as the password. I have to get back to my house before it gets light out.

I can't wait to see you! But don't send any more emails or texts — at least for today — it's too risky. Leave me messages at the blue rock like we used to when we were kids and I'll do the same.

Sarah

P.S. I heard you had Henry Bombs last night. Everyone heard. I'm so mad I couldn't be there. I bet you tried to eat a whole one since we couldn't split it, didn't you?

THAT MIGHT BE THE BEST PASSWORD YET. VERY IMPRESSIVE.

AND SHE'S RIGHT. I DID MISS HAVING HER THERE TO EAT HALF MY DINNER. BEING A GLUTTON ABOUT IT

DIDN'T MAKE ME ANY LESS LONELY. PLUS I GOT A
STOMACHACHE.

THE BLUE ROCK. A HASSLE, BUT AT LEAST IT'LL BE
SAFER WITH DARYL BONNER SNOOPING AROUND. EVER
SINCE THAT GUY CAME TO TOWN A FEW WEEKS AGO,
THERE'S BEEN NOTHING BUT TROUBLE. WHAT'S HIS REAL
REASON FOR TRANSFERRING HERE?

I CAN HEAR PEOPLE IN THE HOUSE.

DAD'S SHAVING, MOM IS MAKING COFFEE.

I BETTER MAKE A SHOWING. THEN I'LL COME BACK
AND CHECK THE VIDEO.

43

MONDAY, SEPTEMBER 20, 7:45 A.M.

PARENTS ARE GONE AND HENRY IS STILL ASLEEP
DOWNSTAIRS.

TIME TO CHECK THAT VIDEO.

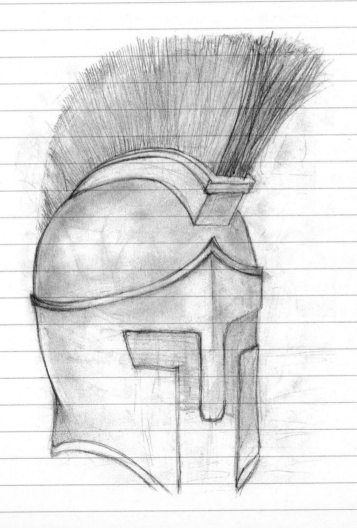

SARAHFINCHER.COM
PASSWORD:
CASTLEOFOTRANTO

MONDAY, SEPTEMBER 20, 8:15 A.M.

I REALLY HOPE THAT ALL LIBRARIANS AREN'T LIKE GLADYS MORGAN. BECAUSE I'D REALLY LIKE, AT SOME POINT, TO WALK INTO A LIBRARY AND NOT BE AFRAID FOR MY LIFE.

IT DEFINITELY LOOKED LIKE SHE WAS TRYING TO HIDE THAT WOODEN CROW. BUT WHY BOTHER? I'VE SEEN IT DOZENS OF TIMES OVER THE YEARS AND NEVER THOUGHT TWICE ABOUT IT. I EVEN REMEMBER THINKING IT WAS CROOKED ONCE AND THINKING SOMEONE SHOULD NAIL IT UP THERE TIGHTER SO IT WOULDN'T FALL OFF IF THE WIND BLEW DOWN MAIN STREET.

IT'S FUNNY HOW YOU CAN LOOK AT SOMETHING AND ASCRIBE NO MEANING TO IT FOREVER AND EVER. THEN ONE DAY YOU SEE IT IN A COMPLETELY DIFFERENT WAY. THAT WOODEN CROW HAS SAT QUIETLY TURNING FOR YEARS WHILE NO ONE PAID ANY ATTENTION.

ALMOST NO ONE.

MY DAD WAS PAYING ATTENTION. SO WAS GLADYS. OLD JOE BUSH AND FRANCIS PALMER USED TO PAY ATTENTION, BEFORE THEY DIED.

I WONDER WHEN THE CROW IS GOING TO TURN AGAIN . . . AND WHEN IT DOES, WHO WILL DO THE TURNING?

MONDAY, SEPTEMBER 20, 10:10 A.M.

HENRY WANDERED UP HERE WITH A CUP OF COFFEE. HE DIDN'T EXACTLY STARTLE ME WHEN HE CAME IN, BUT HENRY DOESN'T REALLY KNOCK SO MUCH AS BARGE. HE WAS STANDING IN THE DOORWAY WHEN I REALIZED I HAD A BUNCH OF NAMES FROM THE SECRET ROOM WRITTEN ON A PIECE OF PAPER NEXT TO MY LAPTOP. SOME OF THE NAMES WERE SCRATCHED OUT BECAUSE I'D DISCOVERED THEY WERE DEAD.

I SET MY ELBOW ON THE LIST.

HENRY ALREADY HAD HIS FISHING BOOTS ON, WHICH MY MOM HATES BECAUSE THEY SMELL LIKE A MOLDY LOAF OF BREAD. HE'S NOT SUPPOSED TO WEAR THEM IN THE HOUSE. IT MADE ME WONDER IF HE'D WORN THEM TO BED.

HE STARTED TALKING TO ME THE SECOND HE ENTERED THE ROOM.

"I SLEEP LIKE THE DEAD UP HERE IN THE MOUNTAINS. YOU?"

I NODDED AND HENRY LOOKED AROUND THE ROOM. HIS EYES LOCKED ON THE DARK SIDE OF THE MOON POSTER.

"HOW COME YOU MOVED THAT?"

"Trying to change things up, I guess."

"I remember one of those songs. Used to get stuck in my head a lot."

And then he sang a verse off-key, which sort of freaked me out. It was the one about the rabbit running and digging holes and never getting to stop. I think Henry was half amazed he could remember the words.

"I can hear that song in my head like it was yesterday," he said. Then he was a little sad — an emotion I'd almost never seen him display.

"Two more days and it's back to the city for old Henry," he went on. "Time to dig another hole, I guess, like the good song says."

"Why don't you just quit and come live here with us?" I asked. "I think my dad would like that."

"For starters, your mother would kill me. Me and my boots and poker and dragging your dad out to the river. Two weeks a year is pushing things as it is."

"My mom loves you," I said. And I meant it.

"I'm easy to love for a couple of weeks. It gets a little harder after that."

He laughed this comment off, but I think deep down he was serious.

I'd never really thought of it that way, but I could see he might have a point. The charm of an old bachelor like Henry probably wears thin after a while. I don't mind him hogging all the time with Dad, but if he were here all the time? I'd mind. I like Henry's loud voice and his energy and the way he can get everyone to play cards. But there's a twitch that sets in after a couple of weeks when it starts to feel like he's almost annoying.

Henry's smarter than he knows, to leave us wanting more and never overstay his welcome.

I decided to ask him a question.

"You ever talk to Gladys, the librarian?"

Henry was leaning against the doorjamb. It appeared he was trying to remember the next verse to the song he'd sung.

Finally, he refocused. "I haven't said a word to Gladys Morgan in ten years. Me and her had a run-in. If I see her coming, I head for the other side of the street."

I THOUGHT THIS SOUNDED LIKE THERE MIGHT BE A GOOD STORY, SO I PRODDED HIM.

"WHAT HAPPENED? WHAT DID SHE DO?"

"LET'S JUST SAY SHE'S NOT AS PATIENT AS YOUR MOM. I STEPPED INTO HER PRECIOUS LIBRARY WITH MY WET BOOTS ON, JUST OFF THE STREAM. SLOSHED RIGHT UP TO HER DESK AND ASKED IF SHE HAD ANYTHING ON BARBECUING A PIG."

"YOU'RE KIDDING."

"NOPE. SHE LOOKED ME UP AND DOWN LIKE I'D PICKED UP HER CAT AND THROWN IT IN FRONT OF A MOVING TRUCK. THAT WOMAN CAN GLARE BETTER THAN ALL THE NEW YORK LADIES THAT'VE TURNED ME DOWN FOR A DATE. SO SHE GLARED, THEN — GET THIS — SHE GOT OUT OF HER CHAIR, CAME AROUND THE DESK, AND KICKED ME."

"SHE DIDN'T."

"NOT ONLY THAT, BUT SHE TOLD ME I BETTER TAKE MY STUPID PIG AND MY WET BOOTS AND GO OUTSIDE AND NEVER COME BACK. I TOLD HER I DIDN'T EXACTLY HAVE THE PIG WITH ME, IT WAS JUST SOMETHING I WAS THINKING ABOUT. THAT DIDN'T GO OVER TOO WELL."

The scary thing was, I can totally picture all this happening. "What'd she say when you told her you didn't have the pig?" I asked.

"She said if it was between me and a chicken and she could only save one of us, she'd definitely save the chicken."

Henry laughed his big laugh again, and I laughed, too.

That Gladys Morgan, what a kook.

I was feeling bold, so I kept going.

"You ever see Dr. Watts?" I asked.

"He's dead," said Henry.

"No, he's not. Mom said so."

Henry scratched his stubbly face.

"I thought he was dead. I haven't seen him in forever. You sure he's alive?"

"That's what Mom said."

Henry seemed a little perplexed.

"Well, if she says so."

Henry looked at the Pink Floyd poster again, and I was sure he'd see it was crooked and want to move it.

"You see that story in the paper about the dredge?" he said.

Henry had been sensitive to my accident there and didn't mention it much.

"Yeah," I said. "They're burning it down."

"It's a shame I'm leaving so soon. Hate to miss the biggest bonfire in three counties. But you know how some people feel about me around here. Probably best if I'm gone when the old relic finally gets what's coming to it."

I know I've mentioned this before, but Henry used to work for New York Gold and Silver. He'd come out when the dredge was running, way back in the day, to keep an eye on #42. He hated what the dredge did to the land, but he was young and ambitious back then. He told me as much. He wanted a big career at a big company in a big city, just like a lot of people.

Skeleton Creek stayed in his bones long after New York Gold and Silver went bankrupt. Some say Henry keeps spending all his vacation time here because he feels bad about

WORKING FOR A COMPANY THAT ALMOST DESTROYED THE TOWN. I THINK HE COMES HERE BECAUSE HIS BEST FRIEND IS HERE — MY DAD — AND BECAUSE HE LOVES THE MOUNTAINS.

I FELT A LITTLE SORRY FOR HENRY WHEN HE PEELED HIMSELF FROM MY ROOM AND WENT DOWNSTAIRS. I HEARD THE SCREEN DOOR FLAP AGAINST THE WALL AND KNEW HE'D GONE TO THE CREEK.

SO NOW I'M ALONE IN THE HOUSE AGAIN, AND I CAN'T HELP THINKING ABOUT WHAT IT FEELS LIKE TO LIVE IN SKELETON CREEK. I'VE BEEN TRYING TO PUT MY FINGER ON IT FOR A LONG TIME. NO ONE NEW EVER MOVES HERE. IT'S THE SAME OLD PEOPLE KEEPING MOSTLY TO THEMSELVES. THERE'S A KIND OF GOTHIC LONELINESS ABOUT EVERYTHING.

YOU KNOW WHAT IT FEELS LIKE?

IT FEELS LIKE THE DREDGE DUG THE HEART OUT OF MY TOWN AND CHUCKED IT INTO THE WOODS. ALL THAT'S LEFT ARE THE GHOSTS WALKING AROUND.

Well, my parents can't complain about me sitting in my room all day. Henry came back and talked me into going down to the creek with my fly rod. I haven't been up to fishing since before the accident and I probably had no business standing anywhere near fast-moving water with a shattered leg barely out of a full leg cast.

Henry did most of the casting, catching, hooting, and hollering. I mostly sat in the shade and watched him work his way up and down the best stretches of Skeleton Creek, hooking fish after fish. I have to give him credit: He'd learned the water and knew what to throw. I've been fishing nothing but Skeleton Creek all summer for years and I've never caught as many big fish as I saw Henry catch today. The guy is a machine.

Being out near the water today made me value it more than ever. The creek is lined with these great big cottonwood trees that fill the air with what looks like snow every time the wind blows. And there are groves of aspen —

THIN TREES WITH WHITE BARK AND GOLD LEAVES —
HUDDLED CLOSE ALONG THE BANKS OF SOME OF THE
BEST WATER. THOSE ASPEN GROVES WILL TAKE YOUR
BREATH AWAY. AND THERE'S ONE OTHER THING, A PART
OF THIS PLACE THAT MAKES IT UNLIKE ANY OTHER. ALL
THOSE BIG PILES OF ROCK AND EARTH THE DREDGE DUG
UP FORMED AN ENDLESS LINE OF ROLLING HILLS ALONG
THE BANKS OF THE CREEK. OVER THE YEARS THE
SURFACE FILLED WITH GRASS AND TREES AND FLOWERING
PLANTS. THE CREEK IS LIKE A SECRET PARADISE NO
ONE HAS DISCOVERED WAY UP HERE, TUCKED AWAY IN
THE WOODS NEXT TO A RAMSHACKLE TOWN THE SIZE OF
A POSTAGE STAMP. THERE ARE BIRDS EVERYWHERE,
LITTLE CREATURES SCAMPERING AND CHIRPING OVER
THE HILLS, AND LARGER ANIMALS RUSTLING IN HIDDEN
PLACES NEARBY.

ALL THESE SIGHTS AND SOUNDS TODAY MADE ME
REALIZE HOW MUCH I MISSED VISITING THE CREEK. IT
GAVE ME A VIEW OF THINGS I HADN'T THOUGHT OF
BEFORE. I'D ONLY EVER HATED THE DREDGE LIKE
EVERYONE ELSE. BUT RIGHT HERE, RIGHT UNDER MY
NOSE, IS THIS SPECTACULAR THING THE DREDGE LEFT
BEHIND. IT MAKES ME WONDER IF THIS IS A PRINCIPLE

THAT CAN BE COUNTED ON: GOOD THINGS CAN BE
CREATED FROM BAD.

I CAN'T STOP THINKING ABOUT HOW THIS OLD TOWN
OF MINE JUST NEEDS A LUCKY BREAK TO START HEADING
IN THE RIGHT DIRECTION AGAIN.

MONDAY, SEPTEMBER 20, 7:25 P.M.

SOMETIMES, AFTER ONE OF HENRY'S BARBECUES OR A MORNING AT THE CAFÉ EATING CHICKEN-FRIED STEAK AND EGGS, MY MOM DECIDES THE McCRAYS NEED TO EAT A HEALTHY DINNER. THIS IS A TERRIBLE IDEA AND ALWAYS PUTS MY DAD IN A BAD MOOD.

"JUST EAT. IT'S NOT GOING TO KILL ANY OF YOU."

THESE WERE MY MOM'S WORDS AS MY DAD, HENRY, AND I SAT STARING AT THE FOOD SHE'D PLACED BEFORE US.

"WHAT IS IT?" HENRY WAS BRAVE ENOUGH TO ASK. HE WAS ABOUT HALF SERIOUS AND HALF HONESTLY CURIOUS AS HE STARED AT THE THREE BOWLS CLUSTERED TOGETHER IN THE MIDDLE OF THE TABLE.

"THAT RIGHT THERE IS RICE," I SAID, POINTING TO THE ROUND BOWL IN THE MIDDLE.

"IT'S BROWN RICE," MY MOM CORRECTED, STARING AT HENRY. "ARE YOU GOING TO TELL ME YOU'VE NEVER SEEN RICE BEFORE?"

HENRY HAD SEEN RICE. IT WAS THE MAIN DISH HE WAS WORRIED ABOUT.

"WHAT ABOUT THAT STUFF?" HE ASKED.

He pointed to a bowl filled with something that looked like green logs floating in a purple lake.

"You really want to know?" asked my mom. "Because you're eating it whether I tell you or not."

Henry pondered his options, swallowed hard, and nodded. "Tell me."

My mom scooped up a big spoonful of brown rice and slapped it onto Henry's plate, then she ladled a glob of purple lake water and green sticks over the top.

"Low-fat yogurt with whole beets, pulverized in a blender and poured over a can of green beans. Eat up."

Henry looked like he was about to barf.

The last item was a flat pan of green Jell-O with sad little mandarin oranges trapped all through the middle. My dad put about half the pan of Jell-O on his plate so there was no room for anything else, and then he sat there, slurping miserably with a spoon.

"Stop that," my mom said. She can't stand it when people slurp their Jell-O.

The best part was when Mom took a bite of this crazy concoction and chewed and chewed but couldn't swallow without washing it down with a Diet Coke. She tried really hard to keep a straight face, but once Henry took a bite himself, just to be a good sport, his eyes started bulging and Mom came completely unglued.

We all had a pretty good laugh and then she let Henry and my dad go to the kitchen and make pancakes for dinner.

We sat there — me and my mom — eating Jell-O without slurping.

"You doing okay?" she asked.

"Yeah. It was nice going to the creek today. I haven't done that for a while."

"I'm glad you went outside. The fresh air is good for you."

I nodded and took another bite of green Jell-O.

"I checked your computer last night," she said. "It looked clean — a little too clean, if you get my drift."

Uh-oh. Maybe my mom knows more about computers than I thought. Was I erasing everything? Was I making it look too perfect?

I pretty much expected what came next.

"Have you been talking to Sarah?"

The big question I was asked in one form or another every day. It should have gotten easier to lie, but the guilt was starting to pile up, so it only got harder.

"I'm not talking to anyone. I just like my computer clean. It runs faster that way."

Mom looked at me sideways.

"Now we're talking!" Henry yelled. He was balancing some king-size pancakes on a spatula in one hand and carrying a handful of paper plates in the other. My mom kept looking at me, but Henry had saved me from any more cross-examination at the dinner table. She left me alone after that, but I had the feeling she didn't

TRUST ME. I COULDN'T BLAME HER, AND WAS WORRIED IT
WOULD MEAN SHE'D BE WATCHING EVEN CLOSER THAN
BEFORE. WITH SCHOOL STARTING IN ONLY A WEEK, HER
RADAR WAS DIALED IN AND SEARCHING FOR CLUES.

IN ANOTHER HALF HOUR, IT'LL BE DARK. I CAN'T GET
OUT OF HERE. IF I GO FOR A WALK ALONE, THEY'LL
ASSUME I'M TRYING TO SEE SARAH.

I HAVEN'T HEARD FROM HER ALL DAY.

I BET SHE'S SENT ME SOMETHING.

THE BLUE ROCK IN THE MORNING — THAT'S THE
SOONEST I CAN TRY TO CONTACT HER.

TUESDAY, SEPTEMBER 21, 8:56 A.M.

As soon as my parents left for work, I crept out the screen door and down the front porch. (Henry snored in the guest room, so getting by him wasn't a problem.) I walked through town, down the main artery of Main Street, passing the twenty side streets that shoot off like veins. It still amazes me that this is our whole town. My house more or less on one end, and Sarah's on the other end, down a street that doesn't look a whole lot different from mine.

I remember when we were seven or eight years old and we spent an entire day trying to figure out the exact halfway point between our houses. We did it because neither of us liked to walk any farther than we had to, and we thought it was only fair to split the distance as precisely as possible. After hours of pacing and figuring and drawing a map of the town, we came to the conclusion that the old station house for the train conductor was exactly halfway between our houses. We would sometimes call each other on the phone and then race there.

She won every single time. After a while I figured out that she'd tricked me by putting the middle on her side of Main Street, not mine, thereby making it possible for her to use a shortcut we hadn't used when calculating the distance.

I think girls are much craftier than boys when they're little.

In any case, by the time I figured out the whole distance problem, it was too late. We'd decided we needed a marker at our spot.

First we found the rock. It took both of us to move it under the station house and center it just right.

"Let's paint it," said Sarah.

"Why?" I said.

"Because I want to paint it. Don't you want to paint it?"

"Sure. Let's paint the rock. Why not?"

This very short conversation says a lot about my relationship with Sarah. She wants to do something, I don't necessarily care one way or the other, and so we do it. Eight years later,

I HAVE COME TO DISCOVER THIS IS NO WAY TO LEAD A LIFE.

IT CAN GET YOU INTO A LOT OF TROUBLE.

IT MIGHT EVEN GET YOU KILLED.

IT WAS MORE OUT OF OPPORTUNITY THAN ANYTHING ELSE THAT THE ROCK BECAME BLUE. IT IS THE COLOR OF SARAH'S HOUSE BECAUSE SHE STOLE AN OLD CAN OF PAINT FROM HER GARAGE. WE DIDN'T HAVE A BRUSH, SO SHE JUST POURED THE PAINT OVER THE TOP LIKE HOT FUDGE ON ICE CREAM.

AND YOU KNOW WHAT'S FUNNY ABOUT THIS? THE PAINT CAN IS STILL UNDER THERE, TOO.

WE DIDN'T KNOW WHAT ELSE TO DO WITH IT. WHAT IF WE TOSSED IT IN A DITCH AND SOMEONE FOUND IT? IT WAS SARAH'S HOUSE BLUE, AND SOMEONE WOULD TELL.

THE BLUE ROCK BECAME THE PLACE WE MET, WHERE WE PUT SECRET NOTES AND TREASURES WE'D FOUND AND CANDY WE WANTED TO SHARE.

WE WERE SECRETIVE LIKE EVERYONE ELSE IN TOWN, EVEN BACK THEN. WE DIDN'T WANT ANYONE HEARING US TALK ABOUT THE BLUE ROCK. IT WAS OURS. AND IT WASN'T EASY TO FIND.

The train still comes through town in the early morning, but it never stops here anymore. It used to, a long time ago, when the dredge was pounding away 24/7, digging up something worth stopping for. But the old station house was already abandoned when we were kids, so we set about exploring it. It wasn't too intimidating, only about the size of a backyard storage shed on the edge of the tracks. It was locked up tight, but the cool thing was you could climb underneath it. The station house was up off the ground for some reason — I think so it was the same height as the train conductor when he came by — and the cheapest way to accomplish the extra height was to put this little shack on a bunch of cinder blocks. Weeds had grown up all around the edges, sort of like a curtain you could pull back. It was cold gravel underneath, and when we crawled inside, it crunched under our knees.

As we grew older, there wasn't much point in meeting at the blue rock or leaving secret notes there. I hadn't been back there in years. My leg

WAS ALREADY TIRED AND SORE FROM THE LONG WALK, AND THE SPACE UNDER THE STATION HOUSE SEEMED A LOT SMALLER THAN WHEN I WAS SEVEN. I'D BE LUCKY IF I FIT AT ALL.

DID I MENTION THAT I DON'T LIKE CONFINED SPACES?

I SQUEEZED IN ON MY BACK AND SLID UNDER, THROUGH THE WEEDS, UNTIL I HIT MY HEAD ON THE BLUE ROCK.

IT WAS A BIG ROCK, AND I HIT IT HARD ENOUGH THAT I YELLED.

ONCE I RECOVERED, I CRANED MY NECK AROUND AND SAW A PIECE OF PAPER TAPED TO THE ROCK. I TOOK IT, CAREFULLY REMOVED THE TAPE, AND TAPED MY OWN NOTE TO THE SLICK, BLUE SURFACE.

THE NOTE I HAD WRITTEN WAS SHORT.

YOUR PARENTS AREN'T THE ONLY ONES WATCHING CLOSELY. MY MOM IS ON MY CASE, TOO. I THINK BONNER MIGHT HAVE SAID

SOMETHING TO HER BUT I CAN'T TELL FOR SURE.
SHE AND MY DAD ARE VERY WORRIED ABOUT
ME GOING BACK TO SCHOOL — I CAN TELL. I BET
THEY'VE TOLD ALL OUR TEACHERS TO KEEP AN
EYE ON US SO WE DON'T TALK TO EACH OTHER. I
HATE THIS!

I'M NOT SURE I EVEN WANT TO GO BACK TO
SCHOOL.

<u>EVER.</u>

TOO MANY PEOPLE IN THAT PLACE.

BEING AWAY FROM YOU MAKES EVERYTHING
FEEL LIKE IT'S FADING AWAY.

I SHOULD BE MORE AFRAID, RIGHT?

I HOPE YOU SENT A VIDEO.

I NEED TO SEE YOU.

RYAN

I READ SARAH'S NOTE ON THE WALK HOME. IT WAS EASY, SINCE IT WAS SO SHORT. IT WASN'T EVEN A LETTER AT ALL. I WISH SHE'D WRITE ME A LETTER, BUT SARAH DOESN'T WRITE IF SHE CAN SAY IT IN A VIDEO.

Hey, Ryan — Miss you / wish I could see you
Password carlkolchak
xoxoxo Sarah

TECHNICALLY THAT'S NOT EVEN A NOTE; IT'S JUST A HANDOFF OF SOME VITAL INFORMATION.

NO PUNCTUATION, UNLESS YOU COUNT DASHES AND SLASHES.

AND WHO'S CARL KOLCHAK?

THIS IS THE FIRST TIME SHE'S USED A PASSWORD I'VE NEVER HEARD OF.

ANYWAY, WHEN I GOT HOME, I FOUND HENRY ON THE PORCH EATING LEFTOVER PANCAKES WITH PEANUT BUTTER.

"YOU DIDN'T GO DOWN THERE AND THROW ROCKS IN MY FAVORITE FISHING HOLE, DID YOU?" HE ASKED.

He seemed genuinely nervous that I'd gotten up early and scared all the fish out of his number one spot on the creek.

"Just out for a walk is all," I said. "The fish are fine."

He stuffed a big slab of pancake in his mouth and gave me his best comic evil eye as I walked past.

Finally, I got back here to my room, so I could write down these words.

Sarah's at school and I'm stuck here at home.

I already checked out that password online. I'm sort of surprised I didn't catch it, but then again, that show aired before I was born. I can't be expected to know every scary pop culture reference, right?

Still, I had to laugh at that Carl Kolchak. Classic.

I wonder what Sarah found?

SARAHFINCHER.COM
PASSWORD:
CARLKOLCHAK

SHE GOT ME.

I MEAN SHE <u>REALLY</u> GOT ME.

I JUST ABOUT HAD MY NOSE ON THE SCREEN WHEN THAT THING WENT OFF.

I SCREAMED SO LOUD I THINK IT WOKE HENRY DOWNSTAIRS.

I CAN HEAR HIM MOVING AROUND IN THE KITCHEN.

BUT IT WAS GOOD — IT WAS OKAY.

SEEING SARAH LAUGH WAS WORTH IT.

THAT'S THE PART I REPLAYED SEVEN OR EIGHT TIMES. WATCHING HER SMILE LIKE THAT MAKES ME BELIEVE WE COULD GET BACK TO WHERE WE ONCE WERE. BEFORE OLD JOE BUSH AND DARYL BONNER. BEFORE I COULDN'T TRUST MY DAD OR SEE MY BEST FRIEND.

I JUST WATCHED IT AGAIN.

SHE'S GOT A GREAT LAUGH.

SARAH MUST HAVE SENT THAT VIDEO REALLY EARLY THIS MORNING WHILE I WAS SLEEPING.

ONLY FORTY-FIVE MINUTES AND SHE'LL BE IN THE COMPUTER LAB AT SCHOOL.

I'M GETTING BREAKFAST.

Tuesday, September 21, 10:21 a.m.

Sarah sent me something sort of scary from school, which I have already watched.

Here's what happened, starting when I left my room an hour ago:

I took my phone downstairs with me and left it in the front pocket of the same hoodie I wore to bed last night. I always leave it set on vibrate instead of sound, and it went off while I was drinking coffee with Henry (unlike my mom, Henry couldn't care less what I drink for breakfast). I couldn't check my phone until I was alone . . . and I couldn't be alone because Henry wanted to play a game of cribbage at the kitchen table.

I was whipping him good, which is hard to do because he's played a lot of cribbage. I couldn't just fold up and leave, so I stayed and finished the game. He came back from thirty pegs behind and beat me in the final hand.

"You lost your concentration right there," said Henry, pointing his finger to the general area where my pegs were sitting

WHEN THE POCKET OF MY HOODIE HAD STARTED TO
VIBRATE.

He didn't know how right he was.

If Sarah had sent me a message, I didn't
care about winning, I just wanted the game to
be over.

"Better luck next time, champ," said Henry.

I wasn't sure what to make of Sarah's
message, which I snuck a look at once I was free
of the kitchen and had started up the stairs.

"Be careful checking that thing," said Henry.
"Stairs require the full attention of a one-
legged man."

I was startled to hear Henry's voice. He'd
obviously followed me out of the kitchen and
somehow knew what I was doing. I pocketed my
phone and turned all in one motion and saw
that Henry had already gone into the guest
room. He peeked around the corner and
looked up at me where I stood on the second
stair.

"I don't care if you talk to her. I think

KEEPING YOU TWO APART IS ABOUT THE STUPIDEST THING I'VE EVER HEARD. I TOLD YOUR DAD THAT."

I WAS SHOCKED. DID HE REALLY KNOW I'D GOTTEN A MESSAGE FROM SARAH?

"WHAT DID HE SAY?"

"SORRY, PAL, HE'S FIRM AS CONCRETE ON THIS. HE WON'T BUDGE. BUT I WON'T SPY FOR HIM. IF YOU WANT TO CALL SARAH, I WON'T SAY A WORD. I'VE ALWAYS LIKED HER."

"THANKS, HENRY."

"YOU OWE ME ONE. I'M SURE I'LL FIGURE OUT A WAY TO COLLECT BEFORE I GO."

HE WENT BACK INTO HIS ROOM AND STARTED PACKING SOME OF HIS THINGS. HE'D BE GONE IN A DAY, AND I WAS SURE GOING TO MISS HIM.

I WENT TO MY ROOM AS FAST AS I COULD AND SHUT THE DOOR.

SHE MUST HAVE SEEN SOMETHING TO TAKE THIS KIND OF RISK. NO MESSAGE, NO NOTE, NOTHING — JUST THREE WORDS RUN TOGETHER ON MY PHONE. IMATSCHOOL

I FIGURED THAT MUST BE THE PASSWORD —
IMATSCHOOL — SO I JUMPED ONLINE AND WENT
STRAIGHT TO SARAH'S SITE.

WHAT I SAW THERE MADE ME REALIZE SOMETHING
IMPORTANT.

SOMETHING BIG WAS ABOUT TO HAPPEN.

TUESDAY, SEPTEMBER 21, 11:00 A.M.

I KNEW IT! MR. BRAMSON NEVER WATCHES US IN COMPUTER LAB. <u>NEVER</u>. HE'S PRACTICALLY NONEXISTENT BECAUSE WE RUN THESE TUTORIALS THAT TELL US HOW TO USE MICROSOFT EXCEL OR WORD OR SOME OTHER EVIL EMPIRE PROGRAM. MR. BRAMSON TYPES AWAY ON HIS OWN COMPUTER, WHICH SITS ON THE CORNER OF HIS DESK. HE'S PROBABLY SENDING EMAILS OR READING NEWS HEADLINES. HE DOESN'T EVEN LOOK UP UNLESS SOMEONE ASKS HIM A QUESTION, WHICH IS BASICALLY NEVER.

SO WHY IS MR. BRAMSON WATCHING SARAH? I'LL TELL YOU WHY — BECAUSE MY PARENTS HAVE TOLD HIM TO. MR. BRAMSON IS SPYING ON US!

I KNEW THEY WERE RUTHLESS, BUT SERIOUSLY — MY PARENTS TELLING OUR TEACHERS TO MAKE SURE WE'RE NOT TALKING TO EACH OTHER? THEY'VE GONE EVEN FURTHER THAN I THOUGHT THEY WOULD. DO THEY REALLY THINK SARAH AND I ARE THAT DANGEROUS TOGETHER? I MEAN, WHAT DO THEY <u>REALLY</u> THINK? WE'RE GOING TO GET INTO DEADLY TROUBLE OR SOMETHING?

FINE.

If it's deadly trouble they want, then deadly trouble they're going to get.

Breaking and entering? Check.

Planting secret cameras at a meeting for a society that appears to be killing people left and right? Check.

Seeing Sarah as much as I want? Check! Check! Check!

I don't even care anymore.

TUESDAY, SEPTEMBER 21, 2:00 P.M.

I'VE CALMED DOWN A LITTLE BIT, BUT I'M STILL MAD.

I WENT FOR A LONG WALK.

I DON'T FEEL LIKE WRITING.

TUESDAY, SEPTEMBER 21, 10:00 P.M.

I SAT THROUGH DINNER AND SAID ALMOST NOTHING.

HENRY LEAVES TOMORROW, SO I FELT SORT
OF BAD.

BUT I COULDN'T EVEN LOOK AT MY PARENTS.

THEY THINK THEY'RE SO SNEAKY.

RIGHT IN THE MIDDLE OF DINNER, DAD EXCUSES
HIMSELF TO USE THE BATHROOM.

THERE'S A PERFECTLY GOOD BATHROOM
DOWNSTAIRS, BUT HE GOES UPSTAIRS AND USES THE ONE
UP THERE. OR SO HE SAYS.

I KNOW WHAT HE'S DOING.

HE'S IN MY ROOM, CHECKING MY COMPUTER.

SEARCHING THE DRAWERS.

LOOKING UNDER MY BED FOR JOURNALS OR NOTES.

STARING OUT THE WINDOW AND WONDERING —
WHAT'S THIS KID UP TO?

WELL, GOOD LUCK, DAD. YOU'RE NOT GOING TO
FIND ANYTHING. YOU KNOW WHY? BECAUSE I'M
SNEAKIER THAN YOU BY A LONG SHOT. I GOT THIS
WONDERFUL TRAIT FROM YOU, MR. SECRET SOCIETY.
YOU PASSED IT DOWN AND IT GOT BIGGER AND
BETTER. YOU'RE AN AMATEUR WITH YOUR WOODEN

BIRD AND FLUSHING THE TOILET LIKE YOU THINK I'M
ACTUALLY GOING TO BELIEVE YOU'RE USING THE
BATHROOM UP THERE.

AFTERWARD, I WENT STRAIGHT TO MY ROOM AND
WROTE A HUGE, COMPLICATED, GET—IN—THE—WORST—
KIND—OF—TROUBLE EMAIL TO SARAH.

Hi, Sarah. I hope you got my note at the blue rock. It was a real
trick getting under there. I hit my head. I have a feeling you knew
how hard that delivery would be for me and chose the blue rock
to exchange notes anyway. Hey, if it puts a smile on your face, I'm
happy.

Speaking of smiling, you were doing a lot of that when you tricked
me with that Carl Kolchak video. Pop culture reference from 80s
TV = Sarah is about to play a trick, dead ahead. I should have
known. Next time I won't be such an easy target.

Okay — the good news — are you ready? I know how to get
inside Longhorn's in the middle of the night when it's closed up.

I've spent a lot of time in that place because Dad runs the fly-
fisherman's club. I know you know about the club, but I'm not sure

you've ever been aware of how often I associate with this group of misfit fishing bums. I don't talk about it because it seems the slightest bit nerdy to be heading down to Longhorn's every Thursday night to tie flies and talk about trout with old guys. At least it comes in handy now, right?

Here's how you get yourself in there after hours:

There is a window in the men's room — I know it's not painted shut because I checked it once just to see for myself. Longhorn's Grange is open on weekdays for all kinds of things, like on Tuesdays when the old ladies meet up and sew quilts in there. And no, I'm not part of the blanket-making club. My grandma was before she died, so that's how I know. I've got a fishing-themed quilt on my bed to prove it.

I think I could get in there tomorrow during the day and unlatch that window. The only way to reach it is from the top of the sink, but my leg is feeling better every day and I'm sure I can do this. Tomorrow night, if you go to the bathroom side of Longhorn's, you should be able to pull that window open and climb inside.

Bring a ladder. The window is pretty high.

Okay, second thing (did I mention that it's getting late and I'm tired — I hope I can stay awake long enough to finish this monster email). Second thing is . . .

The black door on the stage.

Years ago — this must have been when I was first attending the fly-fishing club with my dad — I wandered off from my tying vise and got up on the stage. The amps were there for the bands when they have dances, and I was turning the knobs this way and that. There's a drum set on the stage, too. They just leave it there because it's so hard to move, I guess.

So I started tap-tap-tapping on this drum set and my dad hollered at me.

I stopped.

That was when I saw the black door.

Tuesday, September 21, Midnight

I fell asleep at my desk.

This is bad.

Real bad.

I didn't finish the email to Sarah.

The screen is black on my laptop. It went to sleep a few minutes after I did, so the screen went dim, but I can't be sure that nobody came in here and saw it. All you have to do is wipe your hand across the mouse and the screen comes back on, big and bright, and I'm in huge trouble.

I moved the mouse and it came back up right where I left off.

That was when I saw the black door.

I remember what happened.

I took a break and leaned back in my chair.

I rubbed my leg because it felt like it was falling asleep.

I had turned the light off so it was totally dark except for the light from my screen.

I leaned forward again, placed my elbow on my desk, and rested my head on my hand.

That's the last thing I remember.

A couple of minutes later the screen must've gone dark.

I woke up and it was pitch-black in my room and I decided right then and there that falling asleep was just the beginning of my problems.

The real problem was what woke me up.

Old Joe Bush.

He was in my room. I'm sure of it.

I heard him.

I heard the leg dragging down the hallway.

I didn't dream it! I know I didn't dream it.

You want to know how I know I didn't dream it?

Because I did something then. Something I should not have done. By the light of my computer monitor I crept over to the Dark Side of the Moon poster. The one that covered the words on my wall.

Don't make me come looking for you.

I lifted the poster out of the way from the bottom. The tape wasn't very sticky, so

IT WAS EASY. MY SHADOW COVERED THE WALL
AND I COULDN'T SEE THE WORDS, SO I MOVED TO
THE SIDE.

AND THERE THEY WERE.

MORE WORDS.

WORDS THAT HADN'T BEEN THERE BEFORE.

THE APOSTLE WILL SEE YOU NOW.

I TAPED THE POSTER DOWN AND CAME BACK TO
MY DESK.

DID I WRITE THOSE WORDS OR DID HE?

I DON'T REMEMBER HAVING THE PEN IN MY HAND.

AND I DON'T THINK IT'S MY HANDWRITING.

EITHER I WROTE BOTH MESSAGES OR I DIDN'T WRITE
EITHER ONE.

AND WHAT DOES THIS NEW MESSAGE EVEN MEAN?

THE APOSTLE WILL SEE YOU NOW.

HE'S WATCHING ME.

IT MEANS I STEPPED OVER THE LINE AND I'M NEXT.
THE APOSTLE IS DEAD. I'M DEAD.

I FEEL A CHILL THAT RUNS RIGHT DOWN THE CENTER
OF MY BROKEN LEG, LIKE IT'S IN THE FREEZER AND IT'S
ABOUT TO CRACK INTO A THOUSAND PIECES FROM THE

COLD. THAT KIND OF FEELING DOESN'T COME FROM NOWHERE.

I DON'T THINK IT'S A FEELING FROM THIS WORLD. IT'S FROM THE APOSTLE'S WORLD, JOE BUSH'S WORLD — IT'S FROM THE KINGDOM OF THE DEAD.

I'M JUST ABOUT SURE HE WAS HERE.

EITHER THAT OR I'M GOING CRAZY.

I SENT THE EMAIL TO SARAH UNFINISHED JUST TO GET IT OFF MY SCREEN.

I CAN'T TELL HER THIS STUFF. I CAN'T. IT'S NOT LIKE BEING A MEMBER OF MY DAD'S FISHING CLUB. THIS IS DIFFERENT. SHE'LL THINK I'VE LOST IT. SHE WON'T TRUST ME ANYMORE.

I STARTED A NEW EMAIL.

Sarah — You have to turn bolts on three sides to release the black door, so bring a flat-blade screwdriver with you. Once you get it open, you'll see the stairs going down.

I'll make sure the window is open so you can get in. I'm sure you've got a plan for how to run the camera. You always do.

Gotta go — miss you. Ryan.

I TOOK A CLOSE-UP PICTURE OF MY WALL AND
PRINTED IT OUT AT MY DESK.

HAVING A PICTURE OF IT MAKES THE WORDS REAL.
I'M NOT MAKING THIS UP. I'M NOT SEEING THINGS.

WEDNESDAY, SEPTEMBER 22, 1:00 A.M.

I can't sleep.

Wednesday, September 22, 2:00 a.m.

I can't sleep.

WEDNESDAY, SEPTEMBER 22, 3:00 A.M.

I won't sleep.

I'm not writing on these walls.

It's someone else.

WEDNESDAY, SEPTEMBER 22, 5:00 A.M.

I ZONKED OUT FOR A COUPLE OF HOURS. THEN, WHEN I WOKE UP, I REFUSED TO LOOK BEHIND THAT POSTER AGAIN.

SARAH EMAILED ME, PRETTY UPSET. SHE WASN'T TOO KEEN ON THE LONG EMAIL AFTER WE AGREED NOT TO TAKE CHANCES. BUT THEN SHE SAID IT WAS NEARLY IMPOSSIBLE <u>NOT</u> TO EMAIL EACH OTHER. SHE WAS DOING IT, TOO. JUST BE CAREFUL, SHE SAID — ERASE, ERASE, ERASE. LEAVE NO TRACE. OUR RELATIONSHIP DOESN'T EXIST.

I HATE THE SOUND OF THAT.

OUR RELATIONSHIP DOESN'T EXIST.

HAVE MY PARENTS WON?

SARAH'S EMAIL WENT ON AND GOT A LITTLE BETTER. TALK ABOUT BREAKING HER OWN RULES. I'VE ALMOST NEVER SEEN HER WRITE THIS MUCH. MAYBE SHE MISSES ME AFTER ALL.

I think your idea with the window at Longhorn's is perfect. No one's up there at night, especially around that back side in the weeds, so it should work. I can already imagine the questions if Bonner catches me walking up the street with a ladder at midnight. That's not even something I want to think about. Let's see — 4 a.m. right now. I've been getting by on almost no sleep lately. I think the detective in me thinks early morning is the safest time or something — either way, I'm wide awake, so I'll haul one of my dad's old ladders up there in the next hour and hide it in the brush behind Longhorn's. Not that anyone is going behind Longhorn's to find it.

I have a feeling that crow is going to move again soon. Crossbones members probably check it every day, right? If that's true, then it sure would be nice to watch and see who takes a particular interest in it today. Or maybe we could see someone actually moving the birdie — wouldn't that be something? If we knew who that was, we'd be one step closer.

I need you to do something for me. There's a perfect spot downtown at the café. If you sit at the corner table, there's a nice view of the library right across the street. Just go in there with your journal or something and tell them you had to get out of the house. Marla won't care. She knows your mom, so I'm sure she'll be happy you're out of the house. Just sit there and drink coffee and eat pie and scribble.

I think someone will move the signal while I'm at school. There are only a few days before they burn down the dredge. Whoever is in the Crossbones can't wait much longer. They're just as interested in the dredge as we are — we just don't know why. And Gladys knows I'm snooping around. So does Bonner. They're watching me as much as I'm watching them. I think they'll move it while I'm at school so I can't see it happen.

Let's try to be as safe as we can. Every one of these emails is an invitation to get caught. Leave me a note at the blue rock and let me know what you find out. I'll stop there on my way home and check. If it's anything interesting, I'll leave you a note on the rock and we'll go from there. Sorry to send you running around, but if we're as close to some sort of Crossbones event as I think we are, we need to be extra careful.

Hang in there. Have a slice of pie for me.

Delete! Delete! Delete!

Sarah

I'M ACTUALLY SORT OF EXCITED ABOUT GETTING OUT OF MY ROOM.

I DON'T LIKE IT IN HERE ANYMORE.

WEDNESDAY, SEPTEMBER 22, 10:00 A.M.

I'M SITTING AT THE CAFÉ ALL BY MYSELF. I JUST GOT HERE.

RIGHT AFTER I DELETED SARAH'S EMAIL, I WENT BACK TO BED. THE SUN WAS COMING UP, WHICH MADE ME FEEL SAFER. THAT WHOLE VAMPIRE THING IS SO RIGHT ON. DARKNESS AND EVIL GO TOGETHER LIKE SPRINKLES ON CUPCAKES. IT'S AMAZING HOW MUCH CALMER I AM WHEN IT'S LIGHT.

ANYWAY, I DIDN'T WAKE UP UNTIL AN HOUR AGO, AND THEN I WENT DOWNSTAIRS AND DISCOVERED THAT MY DAD HAD DECIDED TO STAY HOME FROM WORK AND SPEND THE DAY WITH HENRY. HE (HENRY) IS LEAVING TOMORROW. MY DAD TOOK ALL OF LAST WEEK OFF FROM WORK. HE WAS SUPPOSED TO TAKE THIS WEEK OFF, TOO, BUT, ACCORDING TO HIM, "THE PLACE WAS FALLING APART." MY DAD HAS WORKED FOR THE SAME COMPANY SINCE BEFORE I WAS BORN. HE'S A MAINTENANCE MECHANIC AT A PAPER MILL, WHICH MEANS HE WORKS ON A GIGANTIC METAL MACHINE WITH A LOT OF MOVING PARTS. THE MACHINE IS WORTH A LOT OF MONEY. IF IT BREAKS DOWN, IT'S A BIG DEAL.

The problem is my dad has been there so long everyone else is younger or less experienced than he is with this dinosaur of a machine. So if it rattles or shakes funny, everyone freaks out and they call my dad.

"It's amazing they lasted a week," he said when I was down on the porch. "Took two days just to calm everyone down. But I still have time for a Cabela's run."

Yes, Dad had that sporting goods gleam in his eye. I mean, at Cabela's, the fishing section alone is bigger than some of the lakes I've been on.

"You should come with us," said Henry. He was wearing a cowboy hat I hadn't seen before.

"Where'd you get that hat?" I asked.

Henry took it off and examined it with some pride.

"Yard sale. Two bucks. Can you believe that?"

"Did you wash it?"

Henry looked at the cowboy hat as if he hadn't thought of that but probably should have,

THEN HE SET IT ON HIS KNEE AND LOOKED BACK AT ME FOR AN ANSWER ABOUT WHETHER OR NOT I WAS GOING WITH THEM.

"I'M NOT SURE I CAN WALK THAT MUCH," I LIED. A TRIP TO CABELA'S SOUNDED AMAZING AND I TOTALLY COULD HAVE DONE IT. "BUT I MIGHT WALK DOWNTOWN AND BACK."

MY DAD PIPED IN. "I'M GLAD TO HEAR YOU'RE AT LEAST THINKING OF GETTING OUTSIDE. THAT ROOM OF YOURS IS STARTING TO SMELL FUNNY."

THE TRUTH IS — AND THIS WAS ACTUALLY OKAY WITH ME — I COULD TELL MY DAD WANTED A FEW HOURS ALONE WITH HIS BEST FRIEND ON HIS LAST DAY IN TOWN. I COULD UNDERSTAND HOW IMPORTANT IT WAS EVEN IF HE DIDN'T.

"YOU GUYS HAVE A GOOD TIME," I SAID. "DON'T SPEND TOO MUCH OF MY COLLEGE FUND."

I KNEW AS WELL AS MY DAD DID HOW EASY IT WAS TO BLOW MONTHS OF SAVINGS AT CABELA'S IN A MATTER OF HOURS.

DAD'S TIMING SEEMED TO BE WORKING OUT REALLY WELL FOR ME, SINCE I WAS SUPPOSED TO BE WATCHING THE CROW ALL DAY FROM THE VANTAGE POINT OF THE

CAFÉ. BUT THEN HENRY WENT INSIDE TO RUN A DISHRAG AROUND THE RIM OF HIS NEW COWBOY HAT, AND MY DAD AND I WERE LEFT ALONE ON THE PORCH. HE SIPPED HIS COFFEE AND SET THE CUP ON A FOLDING CARD TABLE THAT HAD SEEN MORE ACTION ON THE FRONT PORCH IN THE PAST WEEK THAN IT HAD IN THE PREVIOUS YEAR.

"HOW'S THAT LEG DOING? YOU READY FOR SCHOOL?" HE ASKED.

HE DIDN'T SOUND LIKE HE WAS GOING TO BADGER ME ABOUT SARAH, SO I PLAYED ALONG.

"I THINK I'LL BE OKAY. SEEING SOME OF MY FRIENDS WILL BE NICE. IT'S GETTING A LITTLE OLD BEING HOME EVERY DAY."

"I'M GLAD TO HEAR IT. SITTING AROUND SKELETON CREEK WILL GET YOU NOWHERE."

HE PICKED UP HIS CUP AND LOOKED AT THE DRAWING ON THE SIDE. MY DAD IS VERY FOND OF A GOOD COFFEE CUP, AND THIS ONE, I HAD TO ADMIT, WAS MY FAVORITE.

IT WAS WHITE WITH AN OLD <u>FAR SIDE</u> CARTOON ON IT WHERE TWO DEER ARE STANDING TOGETHER AND ONE OF THEM HAS A BIG RED BULL'S-EYE ON ITS CHEST. THE

ONE WITHOUT THE BULL'S-EYE LOOKS AT THIS POOR DEER AND SAYS, "BUMMER OF A BIRTHMARK."

I WAS THINKING HOW CLEVER THIS WAS WHEN MY DAD SAID, "LET ME SEE YOUR PHONE."

HE KNEW I KEPT IT WITH ME A LOT OF THE TIME AND THERE WAS NO POINT TRYING TO HIDE THE FACT THAT I HAD IT JUST THEN, SO I GAVE IT TO HIM.

HE HAD BECOME A LOT SAVVIER WITH PHONES AND COMPUTERS IN THE PAST FEW WEEKS. THE ACCIDENT SEEMED TO WAKE HIM UP TO THE FACT THAT HE NEEDED TO KNOW WHAT WAS GOING ON OR RISK MISSING SOMETHING THAT MIGHT GET ME KILLED. IN A WEIRD WAY THIS MADE ME FEEL LOVED, LIKE HE WAS WILLING TO PUT IN SOME EFFORT IN ORDER TO PROTECT ME FROM MYSELF.

BUT LIKE I'VE BEEN SAYING ALL ALONG, I'M TWO STEPS AHEAD OF MY DAD WHEN IT COMES TO STUFF LIKE THIS. EVERY TEENAGER IS. MOST PARENTS, EVEN ONES LIKE MINE THAT ARE ACTUALLY TRYING TO KEEP UP, ARE PERPETUALLY BEHIND.

HE TOUCHED SOME OF THE BUTTONS — OBVIOUSLY CHECKING IT FOR TEXT MESSAGES FROM SARAH AND CALLBACK NUMBERS. I'D GOTTEN PLENTY OF CALLS

FROM OTHER FRIENDS I WASN'T CLOSE TO BUT STAYED IN CONTACT WITH ANYWAY. BUT HE WASN'T GOING TO FIND ANYTHING FROM SARAH.

I WAS SURPRISED WHEN HE HELD THE PHONE TO HIS EAR. HE WAS USING MY PHONE TO CALL SOMEONE. NO ONE ANSWERED, SO HE HUNG UP AND HANDED THE PHONE BACK TO ME.

"NO ONE'S HOME AT SARAH'S," HE SAID.

IF SHE HAD BEEN THERE, SHE WOULD HAVE PICKED UP. CALLER ID WOULD HAVE TOLD HER IT WAS MY CELL PHONE. IT'S A LUCKY THING SHE WAS GONE.

HE DUG INTO HIS BACK POCKET AND PULLED OUT A FAT WALLET. THIS IS ONE OF THE OLD-SCHOOL THINGS I LIKE ABOUT MY DAD. I LOVE HIS OLD JEANS AND THE PREHISTORIC LEATHER BELT THAT HOLDS THEM UP, BUT THIS WALLET — I DON'T KNOW, IT SEEMS LIKE THE SORT OF THING I'D NEVER CARRY. IT'S SHAPED FUNNY, LIKE IT'S BEEN SAT ON FOR TWENTY YEARS. ITS WORN LEATHER IS DARK IN THE MIDDLE AND LIGHTER ON THE EDGES. AND WHEN MY DAD OPENS IT UP, THERE ARE ALL KINDS OF TREASURES IN THERE. PIECES OF PAPER FROM I DON'T KNOW WHERE, NOTES ABOUT FORGOTTEN THINGS, FADED PICTURES OF ME AND MOM, PENNIES AND

NICKELS THAT HAVE LEFT ROUND MARKS IN THE
LEATHER.

"HERE," HE SAID, HANDING ME A TWENTY WITH A
FOLD IN ONE CORNER. "GET YOURSELF A NEW SHIRT
WHILE YOU'RE DOWNTOWN. MIGHT COME IN HANDY FOR
SCHOOL."

HENRY BURST OUT ONTO THE PORCH WITH THE HAT
BACK ON HIS HEAD, ALL EXCITED ABOUT GETTING ON THE
ROAD. HE WANTED TO BE BACK BEFORE TWO O'CLOCK
SO THEY COULD FISH THE CREEK ONE LAST TIME. DAD
FINISHED UP HIS COFFEE, AND SOON THEY WERE GONE IN
MY DAD'S PICKUP, LEAVING THE HOUSE EMPTY EXCEPT
FOR ME. I STAYED ON THE PORCH, AFRAID TO GO UP
THE STAIRS TO MY ROOM.

I WAS STARTING TO HATE MY ROOM.

I FINALLY GOT UP THE NERVE TO ENTER THE HOUSE.
IT SHOULD HAVE BEEN NO BIG DEAL CLIMBING THE STAIRS,
BUT I TOOK IT REAL SLOW AND QUIET, LIKE SOMETHING
BAD MIGHT HAPPEN IF I WAS TOO LOUD.

SLOWLY I HEADED UP THE STAIRS, CURSING EVERY
CREAKY STEP UNTIL I REACHED THE TOP. I LOOKED
DOWN THE HALL AND THOUGHT ABOUT SEARCHING MY

DAD'S ROOM AGAIN. BUT I DIDN'T HAVE THE GUTS TO DO IT. ONCE WAS ENOUGH.

I GATHERED A COUPLE OF JOURNALS, SOME PENS, AND A COPY OF EDGAR ALLAN POE'S BEST SHORT STORIES. I FELT IN MY POCKET FOR THE TWENTY MY DAD HAD HANDED ME.

THAT, I FIGURED, SHOULD BUY PLENTY OF PIE AND COFFEE.

WEDNESDAY, SEPTEMBER 22, 11:30 A.M.

The waitress my mom knows isn't working today, which has led me to consume more cups of coffee than should be allowed by law. My hands are shaking. I can feel my heart racing in my chest. This can't be good for me.

Two slices of pie couldn't have helped. That's a lot of sugar. But I can't drink coffee on an empty stomach.

I've got ten bucks left.

How much am I supposed to tip this lady?

She keeps asking me if I want a refill and I keep saying yes so I'll have a reason to stay without seeming like I'm just taking up space.

How does one become a waitress in a dead-end town? I've never seen her around here before. I'd guess she's about twenty-five. Did she move here? And, if so, what the heck for?

She probably married a local who moved back here. She couldn't have known what she was getting herself into.

Bummer for her.

FROM WHERE I'M SITTING I CAN SEE THE LIBRARY, BUT THE BLACK CROW ABOVE THE DOOR IS AT AN ANGLE AND TOO FAR AWAY. TO MY EYES, IT'S AN INDISTINCT BLOB OF BLACK ABOVE THE DOOR. I'VE BEEN SCOUTING THE ANGLE, THOUGH, AND IT LOOKS TO ME LIKE DR. WATTS COULD SEE THE CROW FROM THE SECOND STORY OF HIS HOUSE. HE'S ONLY A HALF BLOCK OFF MAIN STREET, AND HIS WINDOW POINTS IN THE RIGHT DIRECTION.

I HAVEN'T SEEN ANYONE ENTER OR LEAVE THE LIBRARY ALL MORNING. NOT EVEN GLADYS, WHO, I ASSUME, IS HOLED UP INSIDE, EITHER READING SOMETHING HUGELY BORING OR CONCOCTING SOME SORT OF SCHEME TO GET ME KILLED. I THINK NOW IS MY BEST CHANCE TO GET INSIDE THE MEN'S ROOM AT LONGHORN'S. I CAN'T REMEMBER WHAT HAPPENS THERE ON WEDNESDAYS, BUT SOMETHING IS ALWAYS GOING ON IN THE MIDDLE OF THE DAY. I DON'T THINK IT'S THE QUILT-MAKING CLUB AND I KNOW IT'S NOT FLY-TYING.

MY PLAN IS TO DO THIS QUICKLY AND GET BACK SO I DON'T MISS IT IF THE CROW GETS MOVED. I WANT TO SEE WHO DOES IT. SO I'LL SWING PAST DR. WATTS'S

HOUSE AND SEE IF HE REALLY CAN CATCH A GLIMPSE OF THE FRONT OF THE LIBRARY, AND THEN I'LL GO TO LONGHORN'S AND RETURN BACK HERE. I SHOULD BE ABLE TO DO ALL THAT IN AN HOUR. MAYBE FASTER WITH THIS CAFFEINE JUMP IN MY STEP.

THAT TOOK LONGER THAN I EXPECTED. HOW WAS I
SUPPOSED TO KNOW THEY WERE BUILDING TRAINS UP AT
LONGHORN'S? HAVE YOU EVER STUMBLED INTO A
ROOM FULL OF MODEL TRAIN ENTHUSIASTS? THOSE
GUYS ARE BIG-TIME RECRUITERS, SO THEY WOULDN'T
LEAVE ME ALONE. THEY'D ALL HEARD ABOUT MY
ACCIDENT AND SOME OLD-TIMER TOLD THIS REALLY
HORRIBLE STORY ABOUT A CONDUCTOR WHO FELL
BETWEEN TWO TRAIN CARS AND HELD ON FOR DEAR LIFE
WITH BOTH HANDS. HIS LEGS BOUNCED AROUND UNTIL
FINALLY SOMEONE FOUND HIM AND HAULED HIM BACK TO
SAFETY, BUT BY THAT TIME BOTH HIS LEGS WERE
BROKEN.

So THEN THIS GUY SAYS TO ME, "LUCKY HE DIDN'T
END UP UNDER THE TRAIN. THAT'S A WHOLE 'NOTHER
STORY YOU DON'T EVEN WANT TO HEAR."

I HADN'T WANTED TO HEAR THE FIRST STORY,
EITHER, BUT THAT HADN'T STOPPED HIM FROM TELLING IT
TO ME, AND SURE ENOUGH HE TOLD ME THIS OTHER
STORY ABOUT THE GUY WHO FELL UNDER THE TRAIN.
I'M NOT GOING TO REPEAT IT. IT'S A BAD STORY.

Once they had me standing there, I had to hear about the engines and the trains that used to run through town and look at all their models and on and on. It was pretty interesting, actually. I was standing there thinking, ~~Hey,~~ I could join these guys if I didn't have school. I could get my own train and do some research on this and that. These old guys aren't that bad.

In other words, I was distracted.

It was about thirty minutes after I'd left the café that I realized I was away from my post and was probably missing Old Joe Bush himself turning the black crow on the steps of the library.

I excused myself to use the men's room.

Once I was in there, I realized a sink is a lot easier to climb on top of when you don't have a leg that was recently broken into a bunch of pieces. But I was determined to get that window open for Sarah. I must have been in there a long time, like ten minutes, because I had only just unlatched the top window and gotten halfway down again when I heard someone at the door

PEEKING IN, ASKING IF I WAS OKAY, HAD I FALLEN INTO THE TOILET — THE USUAL STUFF.

I SORT OF HALF FELL, HALF CLIMBED THE REST OF THE WAY DOWN AND LANDED ON MY REAR END ON THE TILE FLOOR. IT'S A MIRACLE I DIDN'T HURT MYSELF. THE SAME GUY WHO HAD TOLD ME THE TWO TRAIN STORIES HELPED ME UP AND TRIED TO MAKE ME FEEL BETTER BY COMMENTING ON HOW DIFFICULT IT MUST BE TO GO TO THE BATHROOM WITH A BROKEN LEG, ETC., ETC.

THE FUNNY THING WAS, I'D HAD ABOUT TEN CUPS OF COFFEE AND I REALLY NEEDED TO USE THE BATHROOM. BUT I'D ALREADY BEEN IN THERE FOREVER SO I MADE FOR THE DOOR AND HEADED BACK HERE, TO THE CAFÉ, WHICH IS WHERE I'M SITTING.

I WENT STRAIGHT TO THE BATHROOM.

WHEN I GOT BACK, THERE WAS A GLASS OF WATER AT MY TABLE. (MY TABLE — HOW FUNNY IS THAT? I NEVER COME IN HERE.)

"MORE COFFEE?" THE WAITRESS ASKED ME. SHE SAID IT LIKE SHE'D PREFER IT IF I FOUND SOMEPLACE ELSE TO TAKE UP SPACE ON THE PLANET. WE'D BEEN SHARING IDLE CHITCHAT ALL MORNING ABOUT SCHOOL,

MY INJURY, THE TOWN, BUT GENERALLY SHE WAS A ONE- OR TWO-WORD CONVERSATIONALIST AND THIS "MORE COFFEE?" QUESTION WAS ALL I WAS GOING TO GET.

"CAN I JUST STICK WITH THE WATER INSTEAD?" I ASKED.

SHE GAVE ME THE EVIL EYE, LIKE I WAS A FREELOADER, SO I ORDERED A THIRD SLICE OF PIE . . . AND KEPT MY EYE ON THE CROW.

IT STILL HASN'T CHANGED.

WEDNESDAY, SEPTEMBER 22, 12:58 P.M.

I CAN'T BELIEVE WHAT JUST HAPPENED.

TEN OR FIFTEEN MINUTES AGO WHILE I'M CHOKING DOWN A BITE OF CHERRY PIE, GUESS WHO I SEE COMING UP MAIN STREET —

OUR FRIENDLY NEIGHBORHOOD PARK RANGER. DARYL BONNER.

HE WALKED RIGHT PAST THE LIBRARY, GLANCED AT IT, AND CROSSED THE STREET.

I SLUMPED BEHIND MY JOURNAL AND THEN THOUGHT I BETTER NOT HAVE IT OUT OR HE MIGHT TURN PRIVATE EYE ON ME AND TRY TO CONFISCATE IT AS EVIDENCE. CAN A PARK RANGER DO THAT? I DON'T KNOW, BUT HE'S GOT A UNIFORM AND HE'S A BIG GUY, SO I DIDN'T TAKE ANY CHANCES. I BENT DOWN AND PUT IT IN MY BACKPACK, AND WHEN I GLANCED BACK UP AGAIN, I HEARD THE BELL DING AT THE CAFÉ DOOR AND WATCHED RANGER BONNER WALK TOWARD MY TABLE.

I'M NOT SURE IF IT WAS ALL THE COFFEE I'D DRUNK OR WHAT, BUT I WAS SUPER NERVOUS.

"HI, RANGER BONNER," I SAID WITH THIS SHAKY VOICE. IT SOUNDED LIKE I'D JUST THROWN SOMEONE UNDER A TRAIN.

111

The rest of the conversation went like this:

Bonner: "Feeling better, I see."

Me: "Yes, much. Thank-you, sir."

Bonner: "Seen Sarah lately?"

Me: "No, sir. I haven't seen her in a long time."

Bonner: "You know, she's still snooping around. She can't seem to leave things alone."

Me: "I wasn't aware, since I haven't seen her."

(Mind you, my voice was shaking every time I opened my mouth. No more coffee!)

Bonner: "You're sure you haven't talked to her?"

Me: "Oh, I'm sure. I'd remember that."

Bonner: "Very funny."

Me: "Not trying to be funny, sir."

He looked at me sideways and stood up. I could tell he didn't trust me.

That's all we need — Daryl Bonner following me _and_ Sarah.

He made for the door without turning back, then disappeared down the block.

I drank a glass of water, went to the bathroom again, and stared at the library.

Sitting at the café was making me realize I don't want to be a spy when I grow up. Too much sitting around doing nothing.

Five more minutes just went by and I'm . . .

Oh, no. Don't tell me. This can't be.

Is that . . .

. . . my dad?

He's coming up Main on the other side of the street.

What time is it?

1:05 p.m.

He and Henry are back from the city like they said. But they should be heading for the creek.

Okay, I'm just going to slide down in this booth, watch him, and take a few notes.

He's in front of the library.

Looking both ways.

Now looking off toward Dr. Watts's house.

He's going up the steps.

Has his hand on the crow.

I can't see what he's doing!

He's down the steps and crossing the street.

Coming toward me?

He can't come in here. No way!

Here he is, right in front of the window, about to reach the door.

Hold your breath, Ryan — that always helps.

Keep your head down. Keep writing.

He's walking like he's got somewhere to be.

He's gone down the street, toward my house and out of sight.

That was way too close. If he saw me watching him, I don't know what I'd do.

Or what he'd do.

I can't see the crow. I should have brought binoculars!

Hold on. Something else is happening.

OKAY, THE PAST HOUR HAS BEEN A WHIRLWIND, BUT I'LL TRY TO EXPLAIN FAST. I COULDN'T GO BACK TO THE CAFÉ OR I'M SURE THAT WAITRESS WOULD HAVE BEEN LIKE, "WHAT IS YOUR PROBLEM?"

I CAN'T TAKE THAT KIND OF STRESS RIGHT NOW.

SO I'M SITTING AT THE STATION HOUSE. NOT UNDER THE STATION HOUSE, WITH THE BLUE ROCK, BUT ON THE STEPS LEADING UP TO THE DOOR THAT'S NEVER UNLOCKED.

I WONDER WHAT'S IN THERE?

SCATTERBRAIN!!!! ....

I NEED SOMEONE TO SLAP ME SO I CAN CALM DOWN.

SO HERE'S WHAT HAPPENED IN THE PAST HOUR:

I PACKED UP MY STUFF AND LEFT THE CAFÉ. I'VE NEVER WALKED AROUND IN OUR TINY, HANGING-ON-FOR-ITS-LIFE DOWNTOWN WITH SO MUCH ANXIETY. I'VE NEVER WORRIED ABOUT WHO MIGHT BE WATCHING ME. MY DAD COULD BE RIGHT AROUND THE CORNER. DARYL BONNER MIGHT BE STARING OUT FROM BEHIND A WINDOW. GLADYS MORGAN COULD COME OUT AT ANY MOMENT AND POINT HER SHOTGUN AT ME. AND THAT DR. WATTS GUY — HE MIGHT HAVE HIS BINOCULARS

TRAINED ON ME, CALL SOME THUG ON HIS PHONE, AND THEY'D FIND ME WRAPPED AROUND A TREE IN THE CREEK TOMORROW MORNING.

I TURNED DOWN A SIDE STREET AS SOON AS I WAS OUTSIDE THE CAFÉ AND WALKED AWAY FROM THE LIBRARY, TOWARD THE WOODS. THERE ARE WOODS ALL AROUND SKELETON CREEK, BUT THE CAFÉ WAS ON THE SIDE OF THE STREET OPPOSITE THE BIG MOUNTAINS. I GLANCED UP AT THEM AND SAW HOW SMALL THE LIBRARY WAS IN THEIR MONSTROUS SHADOW. ALL THOSE BOOKS DON'T ADD UP TO A HILL OF BEANS AGAINST ONE BIG MOUNTAIN. I TURNED DOWN A SIDE ALLEY AND COULDN'T STOP THINKING ABOUT A PILE OF BOOKS — LIKE EVERY BOOK EVER PRINTED — AND I WONDERED IF ALL THOSE BOOKS WOULD BE AS BIG AS THE ONE MOUNTAIN. MAKES A GUY WONDER ABOUT WHO MADE MOUNTAINS AND WHY THEY WERE MADE SO BIG.

SO ALL THESE THOUGHTS WERE RUNNING THROUGH MY HEAD, WHICH KEPT ME FROM BEING TOO NERVOUS AT THE THOUGHT OF TURNING A CORNER INTO MY DAD OR RANGER BONNER OR GLADYS READY TO SLAP ME ACROSS THE FACE WITH A COPY OF <u>WAR AND PEACE</u> OR <u>LORD OF THE RINGS</u>. BEFORE I KNEW IT, I WAS

WALKING PAST THE LIBRARY, GLANCING UP AT THE
BLACK CROW AS MY THROAT TIGHTENED. IT WAS A
VERY QUICK GLANCE, LIKE READING A CLOCK AND GOING
BACK TO MY HOMEWORK, BUT THAT WAS ALL THE TIME I
NEEDED TO SEE THAT MY DAD HAD CHANGED THE TIME.

A STRAIGHT SHOT TO MARTHA'S AT TEN PAST
THE KNOB.

A STRAIGHT SHOT TO MARTHA'S AT TEN PAST
THE KNOB.

A STRAIGHT SHOT TO MARTHA'S AT TEN PAST
THE KNOB.

I KEPT REPEATING THOSE WORDS BECAUSE
I'D MEMORIZED THEM FROM THE ALCHEMIST
DIAGRAM OF 79.

BEFORE I KNEW HOW I EVEN GOT THERE, I WAS
ACROSS THE STREET, DOWN A BLOCK, AND SITTING ON
THE CURB, SHAKING UNCONTROLLABLY. I THOUGHT
ABOUT THE MOUNTAIN OF BOOKS AND MY BODY NOT
GROWING. I BREATHED THE MOUNTAIN AIR IN AND OUT
UNTIL I FELT A LITTLE BETTER. IT DAWNED ON ME THEN
THAT I SHOULD KEEP WATCHING FROM WHERE I SAT. NO
ONE HAD SEEN ME — OR AT LEAST IF THEY HAD, THEY
HADN'T STOPPED ME. MAYBE SOMETHING ELSE WOULD

HAPPEN. I STOOD AND PEEKED AROUND THE CORNER ONTO MAIN STREET. I SORT OF LEANED ON THE BRICK BUILDING LIKE I WAS PLAYING IT COOL IN CASE ANYONE WALKED PAST.

I WAITED.

FIVE MINUTES WENT BY. 1:51.

FIVE MORE MINUTES PASSED. 1:56.

PEOPLE WALKED BY THE LIBRARY, BUT NO ONE APPEARED TO LOOK AT THE CROW. NO ONE WENT INSIDE THE LIBRARY. IT JUST SAT THERE UNTIL 1:58, WHEN GLADYS MORGAN OPENED THE DOOR AND CAME OUTSIDE. SHE STOOD THERE A MOMENT LOOKING UP AND DOWN MAIN STREET.

THEN SHE LOOKED AT ME.

I DIDN'T MOVE, AND IT WASN'T BECAUSE I WANTED HER TO SEE ME. I JUST <u>COULDN'T</u> MOVE.

SHE STARED RIGHT AT ME AND I HALF EXPECTED TO HEAR HER WHISPER, "DON'T MAKE ME COME LOOKING FOR YOU."

BUT SHE ACTED LIKE SHE HADN'T SEEN ME AT ALL. GLADYS IS ANCIENT, SO I WAS LIKELY NOTHING MORE THAN A CATARACT-INDUCED BLOB NEXT TO A FUZZY BUILDING. STILL, IT WAS CREEPY THE WAY SHE STOPPED

AND HELD HER GAZE RIGHT WHERE I WAS STANDING, LIKE SHE KNEW SOMEONE WAS HIDING JUST OUTSIDE HER ABILITY TO SEE.

GLADYS TURNED AROUND, LOOKED AT THE BLACK CROW, AND WENT BACK INTO THE LIBRARY.

2:00 P.M.

I LINGERED.

I DON'T EVEN KNOW FOR SURE WHY. IT WASN'T LIKE I HAD IT ALL FIGURED OUT OR ANYTHING, BUT SOMETHING TOLD ME TO STAY. THIS LITTLE DANCE WASN'T DONE YET.

AT 2:03 P.M., MY DAD CAME BACK.

HE WALKED CASUALLY UP THE SIDEWALK AND JUMPED THE TWO STEPS TO THE LIBRARY DOOR.

HE DIDN'T SEE ME.

I WATCHED HIM REACH UP AND MOVE THE CROW, AND WHEN HE DID, I REALIZED HE WAS DOING THE JOB THE APOSTLE HAD ONCE DONE.

THE APOSTLE WILL SEE YOU NOW.

COULD MY DAD HAVE WRITTEN THOSE WORDS?

IF HE DID, HE'S CRAZY. MEET MY DAD, ESCAPEE FROM THE NUTHOUSE.

OR WAS IT WORSE THAN CRAZY?

Was it deadly?

No. I couldn't think about that.

He would've been just a kid when Joe Bush died.

A kid like me.

I walked to the blue rock so I could leave a note for Sarah. Now here I sit with the sun beating down on my head. Stress makes you do things you shouldn't. It's that whole fight-or-flight thing. I worked my leg way too hard today without even realizing I was doing it. It didn't hurt then, but it hurts a lot now.

I hope I haven't reinjured it.

I'm not looking forward to the long walk back home.

The lies I'll have to tell about what I've been doing all day.

The questions about the shirt I didn't buy with the money my dad gave me.

But wait — who's the real liar here?

My dad moved the signal, then moved it back.

Everyone in the Crossbones knew they were supposed to look between 1 p.m. and 2 p.m. on

WEDNESDAY. MAYBE THEY'VE BEEN LOOKING FOR YEARS. WHO KNOWS? PROBABLY IT'S ALL PART OF SOME ELABORATE SYSTEM. THE CROW MOVES THE FIRST TIME AND EVERYONE KNOWS IT WILL MOVE AGAIN AT 1 P.M. THE NEXT DAY? COULD BE. THAT WOULD MAKE SENSE, BECAUSE MY DAD IS GONE ALL DAY EVERY DAY. BUT DR. WATTS AND GLADYS? THEY'RE RIGHT HERE. MAYBE DR. WATTS GOES TO HIS TOP WINDOW EVERY DAY, POINTS HIS BINOCULARS AT THE LIBRARY, AND THEN GOES BACK TO WHATEVER IT IS HE DOES IN THAT OLD HOUSE OF HIS. ALL GLADYS HAS TO DO IS GLANCE OVER THE DOOR SHE STEPS THROUGH EVERY DAY.

Sarah — you're going to have to move fast. Crossbones is meeting below Longhorn's at 12:10 tonight.

I can't walk out here again. My leg is killing me.

You'll have to email me, but my guess is they'll be watching even closer. Send me a note at exactly 9:00 p.m. and let me know if you need me to do anything.

I'll turn in early, tell them I'm tired and not feeling well, and maybe they'll leave me alone.

At least I know my dad won't be home tonight.

My best guess about who you're going to see at this secret meeting? Dr. Watts, my dad, Gladys Morgan, and maybe Daryl Bonner.

Everyone else who might have shown up is already dead.

Ryan

WEDNESDAY, SEPTEMBER 22, 5:05 P.M.

SARAH IS GOING TO EMAIL ME IN A FEW HOURS, BUT RIGHT NOW I'M SITTING ON THE FRONT PORCH, TRYING TO PLAY IT COOL. THE OLD COUCH IS GETTING SOME HOLES, BUT IT'S THE MOST COMFORTABLE PLACE TO REST, OUTSIDE MY OWN ROOM. I HOPE MY MOM DOESN'T MOVE IT TO THE YARD AND TRY TO SELL IT.

DAD AND HENRY ARE STILL AT THE CREEK FISHING, WHICH DOESN'T SURPRISE ME. SOME OF THE BEST BUGS COME OUT IN THE LATE AFTERNOON AND EARLY EVENING. THEY MIGHT NOT BE BACK UNTIL 7:00 OR 8:00, ESPECIALLY IF THEY'RE TRYING TO AVOID ANOTHER DINNER LIKE LAST NIGHT. I'VE HAD THE HOUSE TO MYSELF ALL AFTERNOON AND MOM WON'T BE HOME FOR ANOTHER HOUR. I BROUGHT MY LAPTOP DOWNSTAIRS AT THREE, AND FOR THE PAST TWO HOURS I'VE BEEN DIGGING AROUND.

THREE CANS OF COKE LATER, I'VE FOUND SOME AMAZING STUFF.

I HAVE DECIDED THAT I'M OBSESSED WITH ROBERT BOYLE, ROBERT HOOKE, AND SIR ISAAC NEWTON. AS FAR AS I'M CONCERNED, THESE GUYS WERE ROCK STARS. I CAN SEE HOW A SECRET SOCIETY WOULD BE

123

INTERESTED IN THEM. WHO DOESN'T LOVE A MAD SCIENTIST? BUT AFTER THE RESEARCH I DID TODAY, I THINK I'M STARTING TO SEE A BIGGER REASON WHY THE MEMBERS OF THE CROSSBONES HAVE BEEN INTERESTED IN BOYLE, HOOKE, AND NEWTON.

A BRIEF HISTORY OF THESE THREE PEOPLE IS WORTH WRITING DOWN. FIRST HOOKE. ROBERT HOOKE.

MANY HISTORIANS BELIEVE HOOKE WAS THE FIRST PERSON TO USE THE WORD <u>CELL</u> IN RELATION TO BIOLOGY. THAT ALONE MAKES HIM LARGER THAN LIFE. IMAGINE BEING THE FIRST PERSON TO USE THE WORD <u>PIZZA</u> OR <u>FOOTBALL</u> OR <u>MOVIE</u>. THOSE ARE NOTHING COMPARED TO THE WORD FOR THE BUILDING BLOCK OF ALL LIFE AS WE KNOW IT (INCLUDING PIZZA, FOOTBALLS, AND MOVIES). IMPRESSIVE.

ROBERT HOOKE DID ALL THESE EXPERIMENTS WITH AIR PUMPS AND SPRINGS AND ELASTIC — A BUNCH OF REALLY GREAT STUFF. A LOT OF PEOPLE GIVE HOOKE CREDIT FOR INVENTING THE BALANCE SPRING, WHICH IS WHAT MAKES SMALL TIMEPIECES POSSIBLE. HE THEORIZED CORRECTLY ABOUT COMBUSTION DECADES

BEFORE ANYONE ELSE UNDERSTOOD IT. HE INVENTED
BAROMETERS, OPTICAL DEVICES, MICROSCOPES, AND
UNIVERSAL JOINTS. HOOKE WAS ONE OF THE FIRST
PEOPLE TO ACCURATELY MEASURE WEATHER, TO SEE
OBJECTS TOO TINY FOR THE NAKED EYE, AND SURVEY
HUGE PARTS OF LONDON SO IT COULD BE REBUILT AFTER
THE GREAT FIRE OF 1666. (HE ALSO FIGURED OUT
SOME VERY IMPORTANT STUFF ABOUT ELASTICITY, BUT
I HAVE TO ADMIT I DON'T REALLY UNDERSTAND IT).

ONE OF SIR ISAAC NEWTON'S MOST FAMOUS LINES
WAS ACTUALLY IN A LETTER HE WROTE TO ROBERT
HOOKE:

IF I HAVE SEEN FURTHER IT IS BY STANDING ON THE
SHOULDERS OF GIANTS.

SO THAT'S WHAT SIR ISAAC NEWTON, THE
DISCOVERER OF GRAVITY, THOUGHT OF HOOKE.
NOT BAD.

SIR ISAAC NEWTON IS EVEN MORE IMPORTANT THAN
I REALIZED. SURE, I KNEW HE WAS IMPRESSIVE, BUT I
COULD HAVE SPENT ALL DAY RESEARCHING THE THINGS
HE INVENTED AND DISCOVERED AND NOT EVEN
SCRATCHED THE SURFACE.

From gravity to planetary movements, from calculus to how light works, Newton was at the forefront of so many groundbreaking discoveries it's no wonder he is known as the father of science.

And then there was the last of the three, Robert Boyle, who turns out to be the most interesting.

Let's start with his hair.

The guy had guts to go out on the streets of London looking like that. Wow. Plenty of wigs to choose from at the wig shop and he chose the biggest of the bunch.

Robert Boyle was a scientist with devout religious beliefs. After reading up on him, I think this was one of the key things that made Boyle unique. It's not that other notable scientists of his time had no faith, it's just that Boyle was a Christian first and a scientist second. The fact that he was highly successful at both made him a powerful figure of the times. He admired God's workmanship and saw the study of natural science as a form of worship. The only way, in his view, to discover the world God made was to investigate it. This seems like a sound idea to me.

As far as I can tell, he was a little bit of a nutty professor. Just about everything Boyle ever wrote was short on organization and long on ideas. I imagine, if he'd had a car, the keys would have gone missing all the time. He was

CONSTANTLY REFUTING THE IDEAS OF OTHER CHEMISTS AND SCIENTISTS, AND ALTHOUGH HE WAS OFTEN RIGHT, THIS MIGHT HAVE HAD THE EFFECT OF MAKING HIM SEEM LIKE A KNOW-IT-ALL TO SOME.

HE WAS OUTRAGEOUSLY WEALTHY, PRIMARILY BECAUSE HIS FATHER WAS ONE OF THE RICHEST MEN IN IRELAND. HIS TITLE (I'M NOT MAKING THIS UP) WAS THE GREAT EARL OF CORK, BUT I DON'T THINK HE MADE CORKS OR PLUGGERS OR BOTTLE CAPS. HE LIVED IN CORK, WHICH I GUESS IS A PLACE IN IRELAND. ANYWAY, THIS MEANT BOYLE COULD AFFORD TO HIRE ASSISTANTS, INCLUDING ROBERT HOOKE — YES, THAT ROBERT HOOKE — TO WORK FOR HIM. IT WAS BOYLE'S IDEA TO EXPLORE GASES AND PUMPS, BUT HOOKE DID MANY OF THE HANDS-ON EXPERIMENTS.

MANY PEOPLE REGARD ROBERT BOYLE AS THE MOST IMPORTANT CHEMIST OF HIS TIME, WHICH MAKES THE FACT THAT HE WAS AN ALCHEMIST ALL THE MORE INTERESTING. YOU HEARD ME RIGHT — ROBERT BOYLE, THE ROBERT BOYLE, WAS A CLOSET ALCHEMIST! AND NOT JUST A HOBBY ALCHEMIST — HE WAS FAIRLY OBSESSED WITH IT. APPARENTLY, SIR ISAAC NEWTON ALSO THOUGHT A LOT ABOUT ALCHEMY,

BUT IT WAS BOYLE WHO APPEARS TO HAVE BEEN AT THE FOREFRONT OF THIS VERY SUBJECTIVE SCIENCE. AND WHILE IT'S HARDER TO FIND REFERENCES TO ROBERT HOOKE AND ALCHEMY, SOMETHING TELLS ME ALL THREE OF THEM WERE SECRETLY WORKING IN THIS AREA TOGETHER.

ALCHEMY, I'M STARTING TO LEARN, WAS THEN AND CONTINUES TO BE TODAY A CONTROVERSIAL OFFSHOOT OF "REAL CHEMISTRY." DURING BOYLE'S TIME, IT WAS VIEWED AS VOODOO CHEMISTRY WHERE CHEMICALS AND METALS WERE BROUGHT TOGETHER IN STRANGE WAYS TO ACCOMPLISH OUTLANDISH THINGS. IT WAS NOT "SERIOUS" SCIENCE.

AND HERE WE COME TO THE MOST INTERESTING THING OF ALL, THE THING THAT MAKES THE APPEARANCE OF THEIR NAMES IN THE CROSSBONES MAKE ALL THE SENSE IN THE WORLD.

ROBERT BOYLE WROTE A SECRET PAPER THAT DIDN'T SURFACE UNTIL LONG AFTER HIS DEATH. IT WAS NEVER MEANT TO BE PUBLISHED, BUT IT WAS.

THIS IS WHAT THE PAPER WAS CALLED:

AN HISTORICAL ACCOUNT OF A DEGRADATION OF GOLD MADE BY AN ANTI—ELIXIR.

129

IF YOU BELIEVE THIS SECRET PAPER BY BOYLE, HE WAS VERY CLOSE TO FIGURING SOMETHING OUT — SOMETHING REMARKABLE AND KIND OF SCARY FOR WHAT IT COULD MEAN. ROBERT BOYLE WAS VERY CLOSE TO FINDING A WAY TO TURN GOLD INTO SOMETHING ELSE.

IMAGINE IF YOU COULD CHANGE THE PROPERTIES OF GOLD SO IT WASN'T GOLD ANYMORE, AND THEN CHANGE IT BACK AGAIN. IMAGINE!

WHAT IF YOU WORKED ON A GOLD DREDGE AND HAD A WAY TO HIDE GOLD OR CHANGE GOLD, THEN CHANGE IT BACK?

IT CAN'T BE POSSIBLE, CAN IT? COULD BOYLE AND HOOKE AND NEWTON HAVE SECRETLY FIGURED THIS OUT, BUT TOLD NO ONE? WHAT IF THE SECRET IS OUT THERE AND SOMEONE FROM MY LITTLE TOWN FIGURED IT OUT? A PROCESS LIKE THAT SURE WOULD COME IN HANDY ON A GOLD DREDGE.

IT MIGHT START TO ANSWER WHY SO MANY MEMBERS OF THE CROSSBONES ENDED UP DEAD AND WHY AT LEAST ONE OF THE DEAD DOESN'T WANT TO LEAVE THE DREDGE.

I'M STUCK IN MY ROOM, WHERE I JUST WATCHED THE LAST TINY SPECK OF LIGHT FROM THE SUN DISAPPEAR. SUMMER IS FADING FAST. IT USED TO STAY LIGHT UNTIL ALMOST TEN OUT HERE.

NOT ANYMORE.

MOM CAME HOME AT 6:00 AND MADE ME DINNER. IT WASN'T AS BAD AS I EXPECTED IT TO BE. BUT THEN AGAIN, IT'S HARD TO MESS UP WHEN YOU'RE MAKING SPAGHETTI AND THE SAUCE IS OUT OF A JAR.

WE SAT TOGETHER AT THE KITCHEN TABLE AND WAITED FOR DAD AND HENRY TO COME HOME.

"THEY'RE NOT COMING BACK FOR DINNER, ARE THEY?" MOM ASKED ME. SHE WAS TWIRLING A FORK FULL OF PASTA.

"I WOULDN'T COUNT ON IT."

WITHOUT HENRY AROUND, IT WAS QUIETER. I'M BEGINNING TO THINK I PREFER QUIET. IT'S A LOT OF WORK, HOLDING UP MY END OF THE CONVERSATION. MOM AND I MOSTLY SAT IN SILENCE, WHICH WAS OKAY. WE TALKED ABOUT WHAT I'D DONE ALL DAY AND I TOLD HER I SPENT MOST OF IT AT THE CAFÉ WRITING AND DRAWING.

"That sounds nice."

"It felt good to be out of the house," I said. "I think I'm ready to get back to school. This town is awfully dull during the day with no one around."

Mom smiled. I was glad to make her think I wanted to go back to school like a normal kid, even if I wasn't too sure about it myself. There's going to be a lot of questions about the accident and what I've been doing. I could live without all the attention.

Dad and Henry finally stumbled in around 8:00, arguing about who caught the bigger fish and smelling like two guys who hadn't taken a shower in about a month.

"We're starved. What's cooking?" asked Henry.

"Whatever _was_ cooking is gone," Mom replied. "You're on your own."

Henry and my dad looked at each other, shrugged their shoulders, and went straight for the Bisquick.

"What is it with you two and pancakes?" asked my mom.

They didn't answer. Two old friends in the kitchen making the easiest of all foods. I envied them their time together like never before.

"I was out a lot today, and I'm tired," I said.

I didn't mean for it to sound like I was irritated, especially with Henry leaving and all, but I think it was obvious I saw them as a little club no one else was invited into.

"You sure you don't want a cake or two?" Henry said. "I could tell you about how I caught ten times more fish than your dad did."

"I thought you had to go visit Gerald down the road," Dad said.

Henry nodded, but then said, "Gerald can wait awhile. He'll be up late. Always is."

Gerald is another old friend of Henry's. He lives in the next town over — a town that has the distinction of having been the very last place in America to get phone service. It's even more of a dead end than Skeleton Creek. Gerald is

QUITE A BIT OLDER AND CAN'T GO FISHING ANYMORE, BUT HENRY ALWAYS VISITS HIM AT LEAST ONCE ON EVERY TRIP OUT FROM NEW YORK. THE FISHING HAD BEEN SO GOOD FOR TWO WEEKS HE'D PUT IT OFF UNTIL THE LAST MINUTE.

HENRY DID A LITTLE MORE BEGGING AND DAD NODDED LIKE HE WANTED TO SPEND SOME TIME WITH ME. SO I SAT WITH THEM ON THE PORCH FOR ALMOST AN HOUR, ACTING MORE AND MORE TIRED AS THE MINUTES PASSED, UNTIL HENRY JUMPED OUT OF HIS CHAIR SO HE COULD DRIVE THE TEN MILES DOWN TO GERALD'S PLACE. I WAS SURE MY MOM USED THE TIME I WAS ON THE PORCH TO CHECK MY COMPUTER AND MY PHONE. AT LEAST I COULD TURN IN EARLY AND THEY WOULDN'T HAVE ANY REASON TO BOTHER ME.

I CAME UP HERE A LITTLE WHILE AGO, RIGHT BEFORE THE SUN STARTED SETTING, AND RIGHT AT 9:00 I CHECKED MY EMAIL. NOTHING. I CHECKED AGAIN AT 9:01 AND THERE IT WAS, A NOTE FROM SARAH. IT WAS COOL TO THINK SHE WAS SITTING AT HER COMPUTER AND ME AT MINE, AND SOMEHOW IN THOSE SIXTY SECONDS WE'D MADE A CONNECTION. SHE CLICKED SEND,

I REFRESHED MY SCREEN, AND THERE WAS THE NOTE.
IT WAS SORT OF LIKE MAGIC, AND I MISSED HER MORE
THAN EVER.

I'm so glad you stayed at the café! Who knows what would have happened right under our noses if not for you. This is it, Ryan — something really big is happening tonight. And we're going to see it!

I'm sure I can get into the Watts place while the meeting is going on.

My parents, believe it or not, are out on a date. They should be back in about a half hour. I'll see them when they come home so they think everything is all normal. If all goes well, they'll be asleep by eleven and I'll go straight to Longhorn's, then to Dr. Watts's house. Watts has to be hiding something, and this is our best chance to find out what. He can't be two places at once, so we know he'll be out of his house. I just hope I can get inside.

The tape in the camera at Longhorn's Grange will run for about ninety minutes. Hopefully that will be long enough to catch the entire meeting. I'll start it as close to midnight as possible.

Okay — best part of all — I'll broadcast everything live for you. I can't go live with the Crossbones meeting, but I can use my other camera — the one we used to broadcast live in the dredge — to send you a feed. Go to the site at 11:30 p.m. if you can. That's when I'll start broadcasting off and on. Just be sure no one else is watching.

To get into the feed, go to my site and use the password: maryshelley.

Scared but excited! This is going to be incredible!

Sarah

I'M SCARED FOR HER.

I MEAN <u>REALLY</u> SCARED.

I'M NOT SURE WE SHOULD DO THIS.

I'm really close to bailing out. This is starting to remind me of the night I left for the dredge and ended up trapped inside the secret room.

I hate the way this feels, like I have no control over things.

All I can do is watch while my best friend breaks into two places in one night.

And what if she gets caught? It's not hard to imagine an alarm on Dr. Watts's door going off, or her getting trapped in the basement at Longhorn's Grange. One of those things could easily happen.

I won't be able to do anything but sit here and watch it happen.

I picked up my copy of <u>Frankenstein</u> and started reading it to pass the time.

I'm amazed at how much I underlined and took notes in this old paperback. The margins are filled with little questions and comments. I've dog-eared about thirty of the pages. I went back through, page by page, and read some of what I'd underlined and noted.

<u>None but those who have experienced them can conceive of the enticements of science.</u> This struck me as very interesting, having just spent all day reading about Newton, Hooke, and Boyle.

<u>I shunned my fellow creatures as if I were guilty of a crime.</u>

I can relate, Dr. Frankenstein.

Two years after making the monster, Frankenstein discovers it has killed his brother. This is when the doctor starts to really go nuts. In the margin I wrote: <u>Had he never considered what the creature might do?</u>

A darn good question, if I do say so myself.

Later, referring to Dr. Frankenstein's character, I scribbled in the margin: <u>It sounds as though he is convinced justice will prevail.</u>

It's questionable whether or not Dr. Frankenstein was right about that.

I wrote all over this book in hundreds of different places, like the story and the questions it raised in my mind were too big for the pages to hold. These are just a few of my scribbles in the

MARGINS: WHAT DID HE TELL THEM? HE HAS SET HIS COURSE ON DOOM AND POWER. THE DEAD AND THE INNOCENT, THESE ARE HIS OBSESSION NOW. WAS HE NEVER AFRAID? I AM CONSTANTLY AFRAID. PASTORAL. THIS IS THE DEVIL, I'M SURE OF IT. HE WOULD COMMIT ANOTHER TO THE SAME MISERY. HE HAS KILLED ACCIDENTALLY. THE MONSTER IS INNOCENT, BECAUSE HE HAS NO REMORSE. THE APPLE AND THE ANGEL. ABANDONED. ALONE. IMMORTAL. WHAT'S THAT NOISE?

WHEN I LOOK AT THE MARGIN NOTES, I CAN SEE WHY SOME PEOPLE MIGHT WONDER ABOUT ME. MAYBE MY PARENTS ARE WORRIED I'LL GROW UP TO BE A RECLUSIVE WEIRDO WHO CAN'T BE IN A ROOM FULL OF PEOPLE WITHOUT HAVING HIS NOSE IN A BOOK OR A JOURNAL TO WRITE THINGS DOWN IN. AND THE STRANGEST THING? I HAVE NO MEMORY OF WRITING THESE THINGS. MAYBE I DID IT AT NIGHT, ASLEEP, INSTEAD OF TRASHING THE WALLS IN MY ROOM.

IT'S 11:30 P.M. TIME TO GO ONLINE.

SARAHFINCHER.COM
PASSWORD:
MARYSHELLEY

WEDNESDAY, SEPTEMBER 22, 11:30 P.M.

NOTHING. THE SCREEN IS DEAD.

She's not there.

I wonder when my dad is going to sneak out and if my mom knows he's leaving.

He's going to leave soon.

He might already be gone.

WEDNESDAY, SEPTEMBER 22, 11:32 P.M.

Nothing's there.

This is starting to worry me.

Where is she?

WEDNESDAY, SEPTEMBER 22, 11:35 P.M.

Still no Sarah. Should I call someone?
Maybe her camera's not working. I don't know
what to do!

I'm checking my email.

SHE SENT AN EMAIL!

I don't trust maryshelley. Someone's been trying to hack into my site, in just the last few hours. Bonner? Your dad? My parents? Doesn't matter. Maryshelley is dead. I've beefed up security. Snoopers get shut out and hit with a nasty virus. Whoever it is won't be back. Lost a few minutes on this, so I won't be live until 11:40. Cutting it close!

Use theancientmariner

S.

I'VE GOT THREE MINUTES.

THE ANCIENT MARINER. I WAS WONDERING WHEN THIS WAS GOING TO COME UP.

SARAH AND I TOOK THE SAME ENGLISH CLASS TOGETHER LAST YEAR, AND FOR SOME REASON I OBSESSED OVER THIS POEM. SHE HATED IT BECAUSE IT WAS SO WORDY AND HARD TO UNDERSTAND.

BUT I LOVED IT.

I THINK BECAUSE IT WAS SO SAD AND LONELY.

It's about how bad choices led someone astray. How he can't find home.

It's the story of a wanderer who lost his way and never came back.

I hear my dad sneaking down the stairs.

It's a ten-minute walk to Longhorn's Grange.

Sarah better hurry.

SARAHFINCHER.COM
PASSWORD:
THEANCIENTMARINER

Thursday, September 23, 12:42 a.m.

That's it. I'm calling the police.

Thursday, September 23, 12:43 a.m.

I can't do it.

I don't know why I can't call the police.

I just can't.

Who else can I ask for help?

I couldn't trust my dad even if he was here.

And my mom? Either she's in on all this or she's totally oblivious. I can't bring her in. She'd go ballistic two seconds after I mention Sarah's name.

Henry. Henry can help me. He'll understand.

I'm going downstairs.

THIRTY MINUTES AGO I CREPT DOWN THE STAIRS AND STOOD IN FRONT OF HENRY'S DOOR. I STOOD THERE WITH MY HAND READY TO KNOCK AND THEN THE STRANGEST THING HAPPENED. I HEARD THE KNOCK, BUT I HADN'T MOVED MY HAND. THIS, I FELT FOR A MOMENT, WAS THE FINAL SIGN THAT I'D GONE OVER THE EDGE. SCRAWLING ON MY WALLS, SEEING GHOSTS, AND NOW I'M HEARING MYSELF KNOCK WITHOUT ACTUALLY KNOCKING.

THE TAP-TAP-TAPPING WASN'T COMING FROM THE DOOR IN FRONT OF ME. IT WAS COMING FROM THE DOOR BEHIND ME.

THE SCREEN DOOR THAT LEADS OUTSIDE.

SOMETHING ABOUT THAT TAPPING MADE ME WANT TO RUN BACK UPSTAIRS AND LOCK MYSELF IN MY ROOM. I COULDN'T TURN AROUND. COLD SWEAT STARTED FORMING ON MY FOREHEAD. I COULD FEEL IT, LIKE BLOOD ABOUT TO DRIP FROM A DOZEN SMALL CUTS ON TOP OF MY HEAD.

IT WAS EITHER A BIG, BLACK CROW TAPPING ITS BEAK ON MY FRONT DOOR, OR IT WAS OLD JOE BUSH.

He'd finished off my best friend and now he was coming for me.

"Ryan. Is that you?"

I glanced around and saw a shadow in the doorway. Luckily, I knew the voice.

Sarah.

I have never traveled so quickly and quietly at the same time. Before I even knew I'd moved from Henry's door, I was outside on the porch, holding Sarah. She was shaking like she'd just fallen through ice into a frozen lake.

We whispered in the dark on the porch and I kept thinking my mom was going to walk up any second and catch us.

"I couldn't stand it in there anymore with dead Dr. Watts," she said. "Whatever was outside went left, away from the back door. So I went out into the night the same way I came in. I ran as fast as I could."

"My dad could be here any minute."

"I kept looking back, but there was nothing there. No ghost, just darkness."

Sarah was in shock. She wasn't herself. She was like a robot, repeating what she'd seen with this choppy voice full of air. She didn't understand we couldn't be there on the porch, holding each other.

"Sarah, my dad — or my mom, for that matter — we can't get caught."

"I'll make an anonymous phone call tomorrow from the school about Dr. Watts so someone finds his dead body."

"You're okay. That's the important thing. Can you make it home without me?"

I couldn't imagine getting caught. My parents had threatened over and over again to move away and leave Sarah behind if we didn't steer clear of each other. She had to go.

Sarah reached into the back pocket of her jeans.

"I think Dr. Watts was planning to bring this with him to the Crossbones meeting. Hold on to it, will you? I think it's important."

I didn't want the envelope, but I had to get

Sarah moving. My dad was going to appear out of the dark any second. I could feel him coming up Main Street. I just knew.

"Sarah, you have to go," I said, taking the envelope out of her hand and guiding her toward the porch steps. For some reason I felt like I was pushing her toward the edge of a cliff. I hadn't even noticed she had her camera with her. It was like an appendage, this metal whirring thing stuck to her hand. She carried it around so much I hardly paid any attention.

"I'll get my other camera from Longhorn's later, like around four, before it gets light outside."

I was concerned about her, after what she'd seen. "You should get some sleep," I told her. "You've been through a lot."

She looked back at me all glassy-eyed, and I thought she might tumble down the steps.

"Gladys, your dad, and Daryl Bonner. Those three are all that's left. I wonder what they're going to say to each other?"

"You don't need to go back there tonight," I told her. "Promise me you'll get some sleep."

Sarah didn't answer me. She moved off and got swallowed by the darkness.

"Be quiet out there," I warned, maybe too late. "You might run into my dad."

Thursday, September 23, 1:31 a.m.

Timing is everything when you're deceiving your parents. If they show up at just the wrong moment, everything blows wide open. The close calls add up, until it feels like the end is inevitable. It feels like the truth is going to get out there eventually. The only question is when.

I made it upstairs with the envelope in my sweating hand without Henry opening his door. But when I turned to face my room at the top of the stairs, someone was standing in front of it.

It scared me so bad I nearly jumped down the stairwell and screamed for Henry to save me.

But then I realized it was my mom. Not necessarily a great situation, but better than having a killer standing in front of you.

"What's wrong with everyone in this house?" she said.

"I was just getting some water in the kitchen," I told her. (I hate lying all the time. It's getting way too easy to come up with what I need on a moment's notice. Lying on demand was never a skill I intended to cultivate. Honest.)

"Did you see your dad down there?" she asked.

And this is the timing part I'm talking about, because just then the sound of the screen door squeaking drifted up the stairs. My dad was home. And I could tell that Mom hadn't known he'd gone out.

She was his problem now, not mine.

"Get back in bed," she said.

I think she figured he and Henry had snuck out to have some last-minute fun or something. It didn't matter to me. All I knew was the focus was off of me, I was back in my room behind my closed door, and I was holding an envelope that was supposed to arrive at a secret Crossbones meeting but never did.

Thursday, September 23, 7:15 a.m.

I had a terrible dream last night. Dr. Watts wasn't dead. He was only sleeping. Sarah turned around and Dr. Watts sat up. He'd been using the blue rock as a pillow and he picked it up and held it over his head.

"You're not allowed in here."

Sarah turned at the sound of his voice and Dr. Watts bashed my best friend in the head with the blue rock. The blue rock turned red and I woke up.

I couldn't go back to sleep for a while. There was no noise in the house. It was crazy quiet, which always makes me try really hard to hear the smallest sound. It's a bad habit, because I do hear things if I listen too carefully. I thought maybe I heard my dad's whisper, closer than it should've been from under my door. And I'm almost sure I heard the sound of a marker writing on a wall. Maybe I was half asleep — I don't know.

I'm just glad it's light outside.

There's no word from Sarah, and I'm guessing

SHE TOOK ME UP ON MY RECOMMENDATION AND LEFT
THE CAMERA AT LONGHORN'S AND GOT SOME NERVE-
CALMING SLEEP INSTEAD. I BET SHE WENT HOME AND
COLLAPSED AND FORGOT TO SET HER ALARM. SHE
MUST BE EXHAUSTED.

STILL, IT BUGS ME THAT I HAVEN'T HEARD FROM
HER. I SAW THE GHOST OF JOE BUSH JUST LIKE SHE
DID. IT WAS OUT THERE, AWAY FROM THE DREDGE. IT'S
BEEN IN MY ROOM WHILE I'VE BEEN SLEEPING.

OF COURSE, SHE'S THE ONE WHO FOUND A DEAD
BODY. NOT ME.

WHAT IF SARAH NEVER MADE IT HOME LAST NIGHT?

WHAT IF SHE WANDERED DOWN A DEAD-END STREET
AND CAME FACE-TO-FACE WITH WHATEVER IT WAS WE
SAW ON HER CAMERA?

I SHOULDN'T HAVE LET HER GO OUT INTO THE DARK
ALONE.

A REAL FRIEND WOULD HAVE WALKED HER HOME.

SHE'S FINE.

SHE'S PROBABLY ON HER WAY TO SCHOOL, MAD AT
ME FOR NOT OPENING THIS ENVELOPE.

I WAS TOO AFRAID TO TEAR IT OPEN LAST NIGHT.

I THINK I'LL WAIT UNTIL AFTER BREAKFAST.

Thursday, September 23, 10:00 a.m.

I need to get a few timing issues down straight before I open the envelope. Everything is starting to feel connected.

Okay, here goes:

Last night was Wednesday until midnight and then it was Thursday. The Crossbones met last night right after midnight.

Henry is scheduled to leave in a few hours, also Thursday. Things are going to get awfully quiet around here after that. Good thing I'll be back in school on Monday.

Another story ran in the paper this morning about burning down the dredge. They've moved it up again. It's now scheduled for "demolition by flames" on Saturday afternoon — two days from now, leaving two nights to visit it. After that, no one is visiting the dredge ever again.

I guess my point is that everything is converging. The Crossbones meeting, Dr. Watts's death, the burning down of the dredge, Henry going home, the house getting quiet, me going back to school. Where's Bonner in all of

THIS? I'M SO SURE HE'S INVOLVED IN SOME SORT OF SHADY BUSINESS WITH THIS WHOLE THING. IN FACT, I'D BET MY LIFE ON IT. I CAN'T WAIT TO SEE WHAT HE SAYS AT THE CROSSBONES MEETING.

Now, TO THE ENVELOPE.

Thursday, September 23, 10:24 a.m.

I'm going to just lay this out there as straight as I can, because I don't know what else to do with information this important. What was in that envelope feels like the kind of stuff that could get me killed. Part of me wishes I'd never opened it and that Sarah had never found it. The other part of me is feeling like we're incredibly close to piecing together the hidden past of the dredge and that this is the most interesting and exciting thing that's ever happened to me. I think it might be even more incredible than Sarah and I could have imagined.

There were three pieces of paper in the envelope.

Meeting Notes

- Boyle's Formula

- J.B's trials
  and amendments

- Purpose of the code

- Systematic method for
  reclaiming the assets

CONTROVERSIAL "LOST" PAPERS BY BOYLE PUBLISHED

LONDON — British scientist Robert Boyle (1627–1691), regarded in some circles as the father of the scientific investigative methods employed by virtually all contemporary researchers, has had some of his most esoteric work come under close scrutiny with the publication of heretofore unseen works.

Revealing that Boyle spent many years dabbling in alchemy, these documents, to be published later this month by <u>Scientific Quarterly</u>'s prestigious book division, primarily concern themselves with the scientist's pursuit of turning gold into other precious and non-precious metals, and vice versa.

Reaction from British historians has been consistently negative so far, calling on <u>SQ</u> to halt publication in order to "Protect The Good Name of Sir Boyle."

Boyle's alchemical formula for separating and liquefying gold, as tested and amended by Joseph Bush and Ernest Watts, M.D.

Make a paste of equal parts antimony and stibnite, being careful with your hands and lungs. Deliquesce it, distill the deliquescence, and keep the liquid in a nonporous container (mind the alkalinity!). It will not keep its potency beyond 30 minutes, so work quickly.

Place the rocks or minerals that appear to contain gold in this liquid, and cover with a tight seal. (Be careful not to breathe the fumes at this stage.) After 20 to 25 seconds, open the container. The rocks will appear unchanged, apart from a dusty white coating, much like the coagula of dead ammoniac salt.

Move the rocks to a container of distilled water (must be distilled properly!) and the water will turn dark gray almost immediately. Wait at least 50 seconds (but no more than 80) and pour through a fine-mesh screen.

True gold will remain in the screen, in granular form.

Now grind a small measure of auric seed (granules) to a fine powder, add a drop of the liquid saved from the deliquescence process, and pour the gold granulate on top. The gold will liquefy on contact in working temperatures between 39 and 97 degrees Fahrenheit, and remain liquid for up to 17 minutes. It can be poured into a mold in sections, as it is prepared, until the mold is filled. Wait 30 minutes after the final pouring before removing the block of gold.

So basically, while Robert Boyle was trying to discover a way to change gold into something else, he actually discovered something entirely different. This is kind of common in science, I guess, searching for one answer and stumbling onto another. Boyle never did figure out how to turn copper into gold or gold into iron, but he did figure out two other very interesting things. The first was how to quickly and easily separate gold from anything else, so that gold particles embedded in rocks could be freed and purified. Second, he figured out how to chemically alter gold in order to liquefy it without the use of heat, so that particles of gold could be liquefied and gathered together into larger units without a change in temperature. All of this was done through chemical alchemy, and all of it remained secret, even after the publishing of the lost Boyle papers. It was Dr. Watts and Joseph Bush who thought to expand on Boyle's ideas and actually put them to practical use. Dr. Watts conducted the experiments, and Joseph Bush wrote the paper

AND PUT THE THEORIES TO THE TEST WITHIN THE DREDGE ITSELF.

CLEARLY, JOSEPH BUSH WAS A LOT SMARTER THAN ANYONE IMAGINED.

THE PAPERS GIVE NO DETAILS OF THE ACTUAL USE OF THESE THEORIES AND PRACTICES, SO I'M LEFT TO WONDER ABOUT A LOT OF THINGS. DID THE SECRET SOCIETY FIND OUT ABOUT THESE PROCESSES? DID JOSEPH BUSH USE THE PROCESSES ONLY TO HAVE OTHER MEMBERS OF CROSSBONES TURN ON HIM? DID THE MEMBERS OF CROSSBONES STEAL SOME QUANTITY OF GOLD FROM THE DREDGE? IF SO, WHERE DID THEY HIDE IT? AND WHY ARE SO MANY MEMBERS OF THE CROSSBONES DEAD? ARE THEY KILLING EACH OTHER OFF IN SEARCH OF WHAT — OR WHERE — JOSEPH BUSH HID? OR IS SOMEONE OUTSIDE OF CROSSBONES KILLING OFF CROSSBONES MEMBERS?

ONE THING STANDS ABOVE EVERYTHING THAT FELL OUT OF THIS MYSTERIOUS ENVELOPE — THE GHOST OF JOE BUSH. IT WANTS REVENGE, AND FOR SOME REASON IT'S TURNED ITS GAZE ON ME AND SARAH.

Thursday, September 23, 12:13 p.m.

Henry's gone, which bums me out.

Things are already getting quieter around here.

He said he wished more than ever that he could stay.

"I'd like to see them finally put an end to that thing. It's going to be quite a bonfire out there in the woods. I hope you've got a good volunteer fire department in this town."

This made me think of Sarah, since her dad happens to be a volunteer firefighter. He'll be standing there watching when it goes up. Him and all his buddies.

I wonder if they'll let me and Sarah go, and if they do, will we be able to stand next to each other while the phantom of Joe Bush gets burned into oblivion?

I say this as if he's not already dead. I wish he were alive so I could ask him a few questions.

"Tell Sarah to record it for me, will ya?" Henry asked as he gave me a good-old-boy sideways hug. He didn't seem to remember I wasn't

ALLOWED TO SEE HER. I THINK HE WAS JUST HOLDING ON, TRYING NOT TO GET UPSET AT LEAVING. A SECOND LATER HE WAS GONE, BIG OLD COWBOY HAT AND ALL, HEADING BACK TO NEW YORK. WE WOULDN'T SEE HIM AGAIN UNTIL NEXT YEAR.

TO MAKE MATTERS WORSE, I STILL HAVEN'T HEARD FROM SARAH.

I'M WORRIED SOMETHING MIGHT HAVE HAPPENED TO HER.

BUT HER PARENTS WOULD HAVE CALLED HERE.

SHE'S AT SCHOOL.

SHE'LL CONTACT ME THIS AFTERNOON, I'M SURE OF IT.

THURSDAY, SEPTEMBER 23, 4:13 P.M.

MY DAD TOOK HENRY TO THE AIRPORT AND MY MOM IS AT WORK. THIS HOUSE IS SO SILENT. I TOOK THE ENVELOPE TO THE BLUE ROCK AND LEFT IT FOR SARAH SO SHE COULD READ IT. ON THE WAY BACK I STOPPED AT THE CAFÉ FOR PIE AND COFFEE AND STARED OUT AT THE LIBRARY FOR AN HOUR. THEN I CAME HOME, WATCHED GAME SHOWS ON TV, AND FELL ASLEEP OUTSIDE ON THE PORCH SOFA.

IT'S ALMOST 4:30. I SHOULD HAVE HEARD FROM SARAH BY NOW. WHAT'S HER PLAN TO GET THE TAPE? WHAT'S SHE DOING? DOES SHE REALIZE WE ONLY HAVE TONIGHT AND TOMORROW NIGHT AND THAT'S IT? AFTER THAT THE DREDGE IS GONE, AND ALL THE SECRETS WITH IT.

I'M TEMPTED TO CALL HER, BUT THAT WOULD BE REALLY DANGEROUS.

I'LL WATCH THE HISTORY CHANNEL INSTEAD. THAT'LL KILL AN HOUR.

THURSDAY, SEPTEMBER 23, 8:13 P.M.

This is driving me crazy. Why won't she call or email or throw a rock at my window? Nothing. Just dead air (bad choice of words). My dad and mom aren't talking much. They're taking a deep breath with Henry gone, trying to get used to the silence. Me? I'm smothered in silence! I can't take any more being alone and quiet all the time.

Thank God I start school on Monday. After that I'll talk to Sarah all I want.

We'll come up with something so my parents don't find out.

DARYL BONNER JUST STOPPED BY. THAT PARK
RANGER'S GOT A LOT OF NERVE. IT'S TEN O'CLOCK AT
NIGHT! WHO STOPS BY AT TEN FOR A CHAT ON THE
PORCH?

I CREPT DOWN THE STAIRS SO I COULD LISTEN,
BECAUSE IT OCCURRED TO ME THAT MAYBE HE HAD
SARAH LOCKED UP OR HAD HEARD SOMETHING ABOUT
HER. PARK RANGERS CAN'T LOCK KIDS UP, RIGHT?
THAT'S TOTALLY AGAINST THE LAW.

ANYWAY, HE DIDN'T LOCK HER UP. BUT HE WAS
LOOKING FOR HER. I COULDN'T HEAR MUCH, BUT I HEARD
ENOUGH.

"WITH THE BURN DAY COMING UP, I'M NERVOUS SHE'S
GOING TO TRY TO GET BACK IN THERE. WHY? I HAVE
NO IDEA. JUST KEEP AN ESPECIALLY CLOSE EYE ON
RYAN, WILL YOU? I'M NOT SAYING HE'S GOING
ANYWHERE, BUT SHE MIGHT TRY TO CONTACT HIM IF
SHE'S GOT SOME SORT OF PLAN THAT INCLUDES THE
DREDGE. I SURE WOULDN'T PUT IT PAST HER."

"I'LL KEEP AN EYE ON MY BOY," DAD SAID. "YOU
DON'T NEED TO WORRY ABOUT THAT."

I FELT LIKE A PRISONER UNDER HOUSE ARREST.

What gave him the right?

But I could see why my parents were so nervous. To hear it from Daryl Bonner, Sarah was completely out of control and might drag me down with her. She was the friend no parents wanted their child to have.

If only they knew I am just as involved as Sarah is. She is out in the open, where everyone could see. But I'm lying and sneaking around every bit as much as she is.

FRIDAY, SEPTEMBER 24, AFTER MIDNIGHT

She's out there tonight, doing something. I know it. She's in Longhorn's or Dr. Watts's house or the dredge.

She just doesn't trust me anymore. Why is she holding out on me? Why not at least check in and say hello? I can't understand what's gotten into her.

I've never felt this alone.

FRIDAY, SEPTEMBER 24, 6:15 A.M.

HALLELUJAH — SHE SENT ME A VIDEO!

SARAHFINCHER.COM
PASSWORD:
GEORGELUTZ

NOW I KNOW WHY SHE WAS SO QUIET — AND IT'S NOT BECAUSE SHE WAS MAD AT ME OR HAD STOPPED TRUSTING ME. WE'RE THE SAME AS BEFORE.

AND THE TAPE?

WE HAVE ALL THE PIECES NOW.

AND SHE'S RIGHT — THIS IS OUR LAST SHOT.

I NEED TO KNOW: WHAT IS MY DAD UP TO? WHAT WAS JOE BUSH UP TO?

I HAVE ALL DAY TO THINK ABOUT WHAT A NIGHTMARE THIS IS GOING TO BE. EVEN SARAH LOOKS FRIGHTENED, WHICH FRIGHTENS ME EVEN MORE. I TRY TO LIE TO MYSELF. I TRY TO THINK THAT MAYBE LAST TIME IN THE DREDGE WASN'T AS BAD AS I THINK IT WAS. AND THERE IS THIS PART OF ME THAT'S SO CURIOUS. WHAT'S HIDDEN DOWN THERE?

IT COULD BE SOMETHING REALLY IMPORTANT.

LIKE THE EVIDENCE OF A MURDER.

OR A STASH OF GOLD.

Friday, September 24, 8:23 a.m.

Nine hundred bucks an ounce. If there's even one pound of gold hidden in a cave up on the mountain somewhere, it's worth fifteen thousand dollars.

I wish I could trust my dad and my mom. I wish our park ranger wasn't such a creep.

But most of all? I wish there wasn't a ghost waiting to kill me when I get to the dredge.

Friday, September 24, 11:23 a.m.

Taking a nap since I'll be up all night.

Friday, September 24, 3:15 p.m.

By the way, that georgelutz password was a real find. Sarah really knows how to freak me out. The Amityville house was messed up. I feel like I have a lot in common with George Lutz. I know exactly how he felt.

Friday, September 24, 4:43 p.m.

Daryl Bonner just knocked on the door. I tried to act like I wasn't home, but he yelled my name and it startled me. Nothing like dropping a can of Coke to alert others to your presence.

"Come on out," he said through the screen door. "I just want a word with you."

I swear this guy acts like he's a police officer, which is maybe why I'm so confused about how much authority he has. I feel like he could haul me off to jail and get away with it.

Anyway, the Coke was fizzing all over the kitchen floor, so I asked him to wait. When I got out to the porch, he was standing with his hands on his hips, staring down Main Street.

"Tomorrow, things are going to get a lot safer around here," he said. "But tonight's a different story."

"What do you mean?"

"I mean Sarah. She's just crazy enough to try and go out there again. Why are you two so interested in the dredge anyway?"

Why would he think I'd tell him?

"WE'RE NOT," I SAID. "WE'RE JUST BORED."

"I DON'T BELIEVE YOU."

"I'M NOT SURE WHAT YOU WANT ME TO SAY."

"JUST PROMISE ME YOU WON'T GO OUT THERE
TONIGHT. CAN YOU DO THAT?"

I AM SO DEEP IN TROUBLE THAT ONE MORE BROKEN
PROMISE WON'T HURT.

"I PROMISE I WON'T GO OUT THERE TONIGHT," I SAID.

HE DIDN'T BELIEVE ME.

"TRUST ME, RYAN. YOU DON'T WANT TO BE
ANYWHERE NEAR THERE TONIGHT. JUST STAY AWAY."

I COULD ALREADY IMAGINE HIM GIVING THIS SAME
LECTURE TO SARAH. SHE'D GO ALONG, JUST LIKE I DID,
LYING THROUGH HER TEETH. WHAT GAVE HIM THE RIGHT
TO TELL US WHAT TO DO ANYWAY? HE HAD A LOT OF
NERVE.

I BEGAN TO THINK SARAH'S IDEA OF GOING AT
3:00 A.M. MADE A LOT OF SENSE. THAT'S SO
LATE IT'S ALMOST THE NEXT DAY. IT WAS OUR BEST
CHANCE TO GET IN QUIETLY, OPEN THE SECRET ROOM,
AND ENTER THE FIVE-DIGIT ALCHEMY CODE INTO
THE CRYPTIX.

FRIDAY, SEPTEMBER 24, 9:43 P.M.

DAD AND MOM ARE HOME. THEY'RE SITTING ON THE PORCH DOWNSTAIRS. I SAT WITH THEM FOR A WHILE AND WE TALKED ABOUT A FEW THINGS. MY DAD WAS SURPRISINGLY CHATTY.

I REALLY WISH I KNEW WHAT HE WAS UP TO.

I REALLY WISH I KNEW HE WASN'T A KILLER.

APPARENTLY, DR. WATTS'S BODY WAS FOUND — I DON'T KNOW WHETHER IT WAS BECAUSE OF A CALL SARAH MADE OR IF SOME NEIGHBOR CAME ACROSS HIM. WHATEVER THE CASE, IT'S BIG LOCAL NEWS. (IN SKELETON CREEK, ANY DEATH IS BIG LOCAL NEWS.) DAD DOESN'T LOOK TOO UPSET — BUT AT THE SAME TIME, HE DOESN'T LOOK TOO GUILTY, EITHER. AND IN THE VIDEO FROM LAST NIGHT, HE HARDLY LOOKED LIKE HE'D JUST KILLED A MAN. SO EITHER HE'S INNOCENT . . . OR HE'S AN AMAZING DECEIVER. I WANT TO BELIEVE THE FIRST. BUT I'M FEARING THE SECOND.

THEY WERE A LITTLE NICER ABOUT SARAH AND SCHOOL FOR A CHANGE, LIKE THEY KNEW WE COULDN'T DODGE EACH OTHER ENTIRELY. A GLANCE OR A HELLO WOULD BE IMPOSSIBLE TO AVOID. THEIR MESSAGE WAS CLEAR: <u>JUST KEEP IT TO A MINIMUM AND STAY</u>

179

FOCUSED ON YOUR WORK. DON'T GET TRIPPED UP.
COME HOME RIGHT AFTER SCHOOL.

I ASKED DAD WHAT TIME THEY WERE BURNING DOWN THE DREDGE AND HE SAID EARLY, ABOUT EIGHT IN THE MORNING. THAT BOTHERED ME A LITTLE, BECAUSE IT MEANT A LOT OF PEOPLE WOULD BE OUT THERE AT THE CRACK OF DAWN TO GET A GOOD SEAT AND SEE THE FLAMES. WE'D HAVE TO GET IN AND OUT OF THE DREDGE FAST.

I TURNED IN FOR THE NIGHT AND LEFT THEM SITTING TOGETHER.

SO QUIET, THOSE TWO. I GUESS A LOT OF YEARS MARRIED CAN DO THAT TO PEOPLE.

BUT THEY SEEM HAPPY, GENERALLY SPEAKING. MY DAD, ESPECIALLY.

LIKE THE WEIGHT OF THE WORLD HAS BEEN LIFTED OFF HIS SHOULDERS.

FRIDAY, SEPTEMBER 24, 11:13 P.M.

NEW EMAIL FROM SARAH.

SATURDAY, SEPTEMBER 25, 1:30 A.M.

THE PASSWORD, IN CASE SOMEONE COMES IN MY ROOM
AND FINDS MY JOURNAL TOMORROW MORNING BECAUSE
I'VE TURNED UP MISSING, IS FATHERARISTEUS. JUST GO
TO WWW.SARAHFINCHER.COM AND PUT IN THOSE
LETTERS — FATHERARISTEUS — YOU'LL FIND US.

THERE'S NOTHING LEFT TO SAY.

IT'S TIME FOR ME TO GO.

SARAHFINCHER.COM
PASSWORD:
FATHERARISTEUS

SATURDAY, SEPTEMBER 25, 9:30 A.M.

IT WAS HENRY.

BONNER PULLED OFF THE MASK AND IT WAS HENRY UNDERNEATH.

I didn't even realize the camera had stopped. I think I was in shock.

THAT'S SARAH, WRITING IN MY JOURNAL. WE'RE BACK HOME NOW.

Keep telling the story. Until I turn the camera on again.

THE MOST INTERESTING THING ABOUT THE LOOK ON MY DAD'S FACE WHEN HE REALIZED HIS BEST FRIEND WAS IN THE DREDGE AT 3:30 A.M. WAS NOT HIS CONFUSION. SURE, HE WAS CONFUSED. WHO WOULDN'T BE? IT WAS THE RECOGNITION IN HIS EYES THAT SOMETHING WAS VERY WRONG. IT WAS THE HINT OF AN IDEA THAT HENRY MIGHT HAVE PUT ME AND SARAH AT RISK, MIGHT HAVE EVEN TRIED TO HARM US. THE

WHEELS WERE TURNING IN HIS HEAD, I CAN TELL
YOU THAT.

A SON KNOWS WHEN HIS DAD IS ONTO SOMETHING.

BONNER CHECKED HENRY'S PULSE. HE WAS IN BAD
SHAPE, BUT HE WAS CONSCIOUS. HIS LEG WAS
SHATTERED. I KNEW HOW HENRY FELT AND HOW LONG
IT WAS GOING TO TAKE FOR HIM TO RECOVER. HE WAS
IN FOR A LONG, PAINFUL RIDE.

WHEN HENRY GLANCED AT THE FACES HOVERING
OVER HIM IN THE DREDGE, HE KNEW HE WAS CAUGHT.
DAD LOOKED LIKE HE WAS GOING TO KILL HIM.

HENRY LAY THERE, BROKEN LEG AND ALL, AND
STARTED TO DENY, DENY, DENY. BUT MY DAD KEPT
SHAKING HIS HEAD SLOWLY SAYING, "JUST TELL ME THE
TRUTH FOR ONCE."

AND THAT WAS IT. HENRY WAS READY FOR IT TO
BE OVER. HE WAS FINALLY READY FOR ALL THE
SECRETS TO COME OUT AFTER TWENTY LONG YEARS.
HOLDING BACK THAT KIND OF TIDE MUST GET VERY
TIRING.

HENRY WOULD SAY SOMETHING, THEN MY DAD
WOULD FILL IN A BLANK, THEN ME OR SARAH, UNTIL ALL

THE PARTS WERE FLYING AROUND THE DREDGE, TOGETHER IN ONE PLACE AT LAST.

HENRY WAS THE ONLY PERSON BESIDES FRANCIS AND THE APOSTLE WHO EVER SAW JOE BUSH MOVE THE LEVER AND REVEAL THE SECRET ROOM. HE DISCOVERED THE SECRET ROOM WHEN THE DREDGE WAS STILL TEARING EVERYTHING APART AND FORMING SKELETON CREEK. HENRY HAD SUSPECTED THE THREE MEN WERE STEALING GOLD. WHO WOULDN'T AT LEAST TRY? IN FACT, MAKING SURE GOLD WASN'T BEING STOLEN WAS ONE OF HENRY'S PRIMARY JOBS ON HIS FREQUENT VISITS FROM NEW YORK. THERE WAS NO WAY OF KNOWING FOR SURE HOW MUCH GOLD SHOULD BE COMING OUT OF THE GROUND, WHICH MADE IT IMPOSSIBLE TO GAUGE WITH ANY KIND OF ACCURACY WHETHER GOLD WAS MISSING. HENRY HAD TO SNEAK UP ON THEM, AND THAT'S EXACTLY WHAT HE DID.

IN THE MIDDLE OF THE NIGHT ON A SCORCHING-HOT AUGUST 14 (EVEN IN PAIN, EVEN SO MUCH LATER, HE REMEMBERED THE DATE), HENRY GOT IN THE LAKE OF WATER THE DREDGE FLOATED IN, SWAM OVER AMID THE POUNDING NOISE, AND BOARDED. DRIPPING WET FROM

HEAD TO TOE, HE WATCHED AS OLD JOE BUSH MOVED A HANDLE THAT DIDN'T SEEM TO HAVE ANY PURPOSE.

THE THING THAT MADE ME THE MOST ANGRY THE WHOLE TIME HENRY WAS TALKING ABOUT THIS WAS THAT IT SEEMED LIKE HE'D NEVER, EVER LIKED SKELETON CREEK OR ANYONE IN IT. FROM BEGINNING TO END, THAT HAD ALWAYS BEEN AN ACT.

THIS, FOR ME, WAS AN UNFORGIVABLE DECEPTION.

He only came back again and again for one reason.

YOU GOT IT, SARAH. GOLD.

It was only _ever_ about getting his greedy hands on the gold.

BUT FINDING THE SECRET ROOM WAS ONLY PART OF THE PUZZLE. IT WOULD TAKE A LOT MORE THAN THAT TO GET WHAT HE WANTED, BECAUSE OLD JOE BUSH WAS A REALLY SMART GUY WHO LOVED SKELETON CREEK.

Henry didn't actually say this. We figured it out this morning. We haven't slept. And Ryan's dad finally started talking.

YEAH. JOE BUSH CREATED LAYERS OF SECRECY WITHIN AN ORGANIZATION HE FOUNDED WHEN THE DREDGE SHOWED UP IN TOWN: THE CROSSBONES. ITS CHARTER MEMBERS WERE THE THREE MEN WHO WORKED THE NIGHT SHIFT TOGETHER ON THE DREDGE: JOE BUSH, THE APOSTLE, AND FRANCIS PALMER. ONLY THOSE THREE WERE AWARE OF THE LOCATION — OR EVEN THE EXISTENCE — OF THE SECRET ROOM. THE THREE WERE ABSOLUTELY SWORN TO SECRECY, AND TOGETHER THEY RECRUITED DR. WATTS, GLADYS MORGAN, AND MY DAD, PAUL MCCRAY.

DR. WATTS AND JOE CREATED THE FORMULAS FOR PURIFYING AND MELTING GOLD, BUT DR. WATTS NEVER KNEW ANYTHING ABOUT A SECRET ROOM. HE WAS CONTENT TO DO THE CHEMISTRY WITH JOE AND KEEP OUT OF THE DIRTY DETAILS OF STEALING GOLD. JOE GAVE THE COMBINATION TO THE CRYPTIX TO MY DAD AND GLADYS BUT NO ONE ELSE. THEY HAD NO IDEA A SECRET ROOM HAD BEEN CREATED OR EVEN WHY.

And everyone in the Crossbones was given one primary objective: to save the town from the evil of the Dredge. In due time, when Joe was ready, all the members would know every secret. But he knew that would have to wait a long time, at least until the Dredge was shut down for good.

There was one big problem. Old Joe Bush might have been smart as a whip, but he wasn't impervious to accidents. According to Henry (but then, how much can we really trust him?), Old Joe Bush really did die by accident. He really <u>was</u> pulled into the gears by the cuff on his pants. His leg was smashed and the gears spit him out into the water below, just like the legend said. And it happened the night after Henry discovered the secret room.

Only Joe knew every important detail: the existence of the secret room he'd made, where it was, the combination to unlock the cryptix, and the alchemy formula for processing gold the way he'd secretly done it.

HENRY WENT STRAIGHT TO FRANCIS PALMER
WHEN HE COULD NO LONGER TURN TO JOE FOR
ANSWERS. HE THREATENED FRANCIS WITH LOSING
HIS JOB. BUT FRANCIS DIDN'T KNOW ANYTHING
HENRY DIDN'T ALREADY KNOW. HE KNEW JOE
SPENT HOURS AND HOURS IN THE SECRET ROOM. HE
KNEW WHERE THE SECRET ROOM WAS. BUT THAT
WAS IT.

SO HENRY QUESTIONED FRANCIS MERCILESSLY
AND — AS HE TOLD IT — <u>ACCIDENTALLY</u> KILLED HIM.
THE SAME WAS TRUE FOR THE APOSTLE.

HENRY SAID IT SOMETHING LIKE THIS:

"THEY WERE ALL ACCIDENTS! I NEVER MEANT
TO HURT ANYONE. I SCUFFLED WITH FRANCIS UP THERE
AND HE FELL. AND THAT CRAZY APOSTLE, I DUNKED
HIM IN THE RIVER BUT I DIDN'T DROWN HIM. HE
JUST SLIPPED OUT OF MY HANDS AND DRIFTED
DOWNSTREAM IN THE DARK. IT WASN'T MY FAULT HE
COULDN'T SWIM."

AS FAR AS HENRY WAS CONCERNED, VERY LITTLE
WAS EVER HIS FAULT.

AFTER THE APOSTLE DIED, THE REMAINING
MEMBERS OF THE CROSSBONES FELL QUIET FOR

YEARS. DR. WATTS, GLADYS, AND MY DAD ALL WENT ON WITH THEIR DAILY LIVES. BETWEEN THE THREE OF THEM, THEY HAD NO IDEA A SECRET ROOM EVEN EXISTED. THEY ONLY HAD A HUNCH THERE WAS SOME GOLD HIDDEN SOMEWHERE AND THAT SOMEONE HAD KILLED THEIR FRIENDS IN SEARCH OF IT. BEST TO LEAVE WELL ENOUGH ALONE.

YEAR AFTER YEAR, HENRY CAME BACK, SEARCHING FOR CLUES. HE WAS SURE THERE WAS A STASH OF GOLD HIDDEN SOMEWHERE ON THE MOUNTAIN, AND HE WAS CONVINCED THE CRYPTIX CONTAINED A MAP THAT WOULD TELL HIM WHERE TO LOOK. IF ONLY HE COULD UNLOCK IT WITHOUT BLOWING HIMSELF UP.

ON ONE OF HENRY'S VISITS SOME KIDS WERE SNEAKING AROUND THE DREDGE AND HE CHASED THEM OFF. AFTER THAT HE NEEDED A PLAN TO KEEP SNOOPING THRILL-SEEKERS AWAY FROM THE DREDGE. SO HE CREATED THE GHOST OF JOE BUSH. ELEVEN MONTHS OUT OF EVERY YEAR IN NEW YORK GAVE HIM PLENTY OF TIME TO FIGURE THINGS OUT. EVERY YEAR HE ADDED A FEW MORE SUBTLE TOUCHES. UNDERGROUND SPEAKERS, REMOTE SWITCHES FOR

SOUNDS, IRIDESCENT MASKS AND HOODS, INVISIBLE TRIP WIRES THAT LET HIM KNOW WHEN SOMEONE WAS HEADING DOWN THE TRAIL TOWARD THE DREDGE. HE EVEN HAD HIS OWN SECRET SHORTCUT THROUGH A SEEMINGLY IMPENETRABLE FORTRESS OF BLACKBERRY BUSHES.

THINGS WERE DIFFERENT WITH ME AND SARAH. NUMBER ONE, WE WERE PERSISTENT.

I was persistent. What's this __we__ stuff?

LIKE I WAS SAYING, __WE__ WERE PERSISTENT. BUT THERE WAS ONE THING THAT TIPPED HENRY OFF THAT I DIDN'T KNOW ABOUT UNTIL HE MENTIONED IT. SARAH HAD BEEN GOING TO THE DREDGE AND FILMING IT FOR WEEKS BEFORE THAT FIRST VIDEO SHE SHOWED ME. SHE'D ALREADY BEEN INSIDE, ALREADY SCOUTED AROUND FOR HOURS. AND HERE'S ONE OF THE WEIRDEST PARTS OF THE WHOLE STORY: HENRY HAD SURVEILLANCE CAMERAS SET UP INSIDE AND OUTSIDE THE DREDGE. NOT ONLY COULD HE KEEP AN EYE ON IT FROM A LAPTOP HE CARRIED WITH HIM, HE COULD ALSO WATCH IT FROM NEW YORK. AND WATCH IT HE DID. YEARS OF

WATCHING THE DREDGE TURNED HENRY INTO QUITE THE
TECHNICIAN WITH THIS SORT OF THING. IF A PERSON
WALKED PAST CERTAIN PLACES IN THE WOODS ON THE
WAY TO THE DREDGE, THEY UNKNOWINGLY SET OFF
ALERTS ALL THE WAY OUT IN NEW YORK. THE BEST
I CAN UNDERSTAND IT, THERE WERE WIDE PADS BURIED A
FOOT UNDERGROUND AND THEY WERE SENSITIVE TO
PRESSURE. IF SOMEONE WALKED ON THE TRAIL, HENRY
KNEW THEY WERE COMING.

AND SO IT WAS THAT BY THE TIME HENRY
ARRIVED IN SKELETON CREEK, HE'D WATCHED SARAH
WITH HER CAMERA. HE'D SEEN HER VISITING THE
DREDGE NOT ONCE BUT SEVERAL TIMES, RECORDING ALL
KINDS OF THINGS. IT WORRIED HIM ENOUGH TO PUT HIS
WELL-WORN SCARE TACTICS INTO HIGH GEAR WHEN HE
SHOWED UP IN SKELETON CREEK.

*Henry was also growing bolder because of all the
talk about burning down the dredge.*

HE DIDN'T KNOW WHO ELSE WAS IN THE
CROSSBONES, BUT HE WAS SURE THERE WERE OTHERS.
HE'D SEEN LITTLE HINTS HERE AND THERE FROM MY

DAD. AND THERE WAS THAT ONE NIGHT, WHEN I FELL ASLEEP AT MY DESK AND WOKE UP WITH WORDS SCRIBBLED ON MY WALL WITH A PEN. I HAD THAT LIST — THE LIST OF EVERYONE WE'D DISCOVERED WAS IN THE CROSSBONES. IT WAS THAT LIST THAT SENT HENRY TO SEE DR. WATTS WHEN HE SAID HE WAS VISITING A FRIEND.

HE HAD AN EXCUSE FOR THAT NIGHT, TOO.

"I DIDN'T MEAN TO KILL DR. WATTS. I FORCED MY WAY IN, THAT MUCH IS TRUE. AND I QUESTIONED HIM. I KNEW HE HAD ANSWERS, BUT THE OLD LOON WOULDN'T TELL ME ANYTHING. I ONLY SWUNG ONE TIME, CAUGHT HIM RIGHT IN THE HEAD. BUT HE MADE ME SO MAD, ALL CLAMMED UP LIKE THAT. HE WAS FRAIL, MORE SO THAN I REALIZED. I'M SURE HE DIED OF A HEART ATTACK, NOT THAT LITTLE BUMP ON HIS HEAD."

I GUESS YOU COULD SAY HENRY'S CONFESSION WAS TEMPERED WITH QUITE A LOT OF EXCUSES. AT LEAST HE DIDN'T DO MUCH COMPLAINING WHEN IT CAME TO HIS OWN SEVERE INJURIES.

"DID YOU WRITE THOSE WORDS ON MY WALL?" I ASKED HIM.

"WHAT WORDS? WHAT ARE YOU TALKING

ABOUT?" DAD ASKED. HE WAS ALREADY MAD, BUT THE
IDEA OF HENRY IN MY ROOM, WRITING ON MY WALLS,
BROUGHT HIS ANGER TO ANOTHER LEVEL.

HENRY JUST LOOKED DOWN AT HIS BROKEN LEGS
AND WOULDN'T ANSWER. HE COULDN'T BRING HIMSELF
TO LOOK AT MY DAD, AND I NEVER KNEW FOR SURE
IF IT HAD BEEN HENRY OR NOT.

FINALLY, HENRY JUST ABOUT PASSED OUT FROM
THE PAIN. BONNER CALLED THE HOSPITAL FOR AN
AMBULANCE.

And I got the camera working again.

THERE WAS AT LEAST ONE MORE BIG SURPRISE
WAITING FOR US ON THE DREDGE. BUT THIS PART IS
BETTER SEEN THAN SAID.

WEDNESDAY, SEPTEMBER 29, 4:30 P.M.

I'M BACK IN MY ROOM ALONE. I BEGAN WRITING THINGS DOWN IN HERE, SO IT SEEMS LIKE THE MOST LOGICAL PLACE TO END UP.

IN SOME WAYS I'M MORE AFRAID THAN I WAS WHEN THIS WHOLE THING STARTED. THE DANGER HAD ALWAYS FELT AS IF IT CREPT OFF THE PAGE OF A SCARY STORY I'D MADE UP IN MY HEAD. SURE, IT WAS SPOOKY OUT ON THE DREDGE, BUT THERE WAS A FEELING SOMEWHERE AT THE BACK OF MY MIND THAT IT WAS STILL A GHOST STORY.

THINGS ARE DIFFERENT NOW.

HENRY IS OUT THERE SOMEWHERE. THEY SEARCHED THE WOODS FOR DAYS AND FOUND NOTHING. CHANCES ARE HE PLANNED FOR THIS AND CREATED A SECRET WAY TO ESCAPE UNNOTICED. IT WOULD BE JUST LIKE HIM TO THINK AHEAD. I WONDER WHAT HIS APARTMENT IS LIKE IN NEW YORK — FULL OF CAMERAS POINTED AT THE DREDGE — WATCHING THEM REMOVE ALL THE HIDDEN TREASURES. I DON'T KNOW AND NEITHER DOES HENRY, BECAUSE HE'S VANISHED INTO THIN AIR. NO ONE HAS BEEN ABLE TO FIND HIM.

WE'VE TAKEN HIS GOLD AND LEFT HIM INJURED. HE

HATES US. AND THE WORST PART, HENRY THINKS I'M THE CAUSE OF ALL HIS PROBLEMS.

FROM HERE ON OUT THE DANGER IS REAL.

I'M GOING TO CHANGE SUBJECTS BECAUSE I'M HOPING IT WILL MAKE ME FEEL BETTER.

RIGHT AFTER I PULLED UP THAT FLOORBOARD ON THE DREDGE AND DUMPED THE BLOCKS OF GOLD OUT, DARYL TOLD US SOMETHING WE DIDN'T KNOW ABOUT HIS DAD. PART OF ME FEELS LIKE WE SHOULD HAVE FIGURED IT OUT ON OUR OWN A LONG TIME AGO, BUT WE NEVER SUSPECTED.

"YOU DON'T KNOW WHO I AM, DO YOU?" HE ASKED US.

IT WAS SARAH WHO STARTED CHIPPING AWAY AT THE OPTIONS.

"YOU'RE NOT A PART OF THE CROSSBONES. YOU DIDN'T HAUNT THIS PLACE. YOU'VE NEVER BEEN HERE BEFORE THIS SUMMER. WHO ARE YOU?"

"I'VE ALWAYS SUSPECTED FOUL PLAY," SAID DARYL. "ALWAYS. BUT I NEVER IMAGINED . . ."

"WHO ARE YOU?" SARAH REPEATED.

"I WAS A FOSTER KID IN THE CITY UNTIL I WAS TWELVE. THAT'S WHEN THE BONNERS ADOPTED ME.

197

About a year after that I started going by my middle name — Daryl. I guess I was looking for a break with the past. A fresh start."

"What's your first name?" asked Sarah. She could make a really good investigative reporter. Always first with the questions.

"Joseph," said Daryl. "I'm Old Joe Bush's son."

I remember feeling light-headed for some reason, like the ghost of Joe Bush had inhabited his son and we were about to be appropriately scared out of our wits. But the moment passed and I realized something as Daryl went on. The guy had lost his dad to the dredge. He'd obviously lost his mom young, too, and he'd been through the toughest kind of childhood. But curiosity had gotten the better of him. He'd been searching for answers just like we had, only the stakes were even higher.

"Now I know the truth," he said, looking at the opening to the secret room.

All this happened before we realized we'd basically forgotten all about the cryptix and

198

THE SECRETS WE'D UNCOVERED. AFTER WE FIGURED OUT JOE HAD LIQUEFIED THE GOLD AND HIDDEN IT INSIDE THE PLANKS OF THE DREDGE ITSELF, DARYL PIPED BACK IN.

"I SHOULD HAVE GUESSED HE WOULD COME UP WITH SOMETHING LIKE THIS. MY DAD WAS ABOUT THE HANDIEST GUY IN TOWN, EVERYBODY SAID THAT. THAT'S WHY THEY CHOSE HIM TO RUN THE DREDGE. HE WAS GIFTED WITH MOTORS AND CRANKS AND ALL KINDS OF MACHINERY. BUT HE WAS ALSO A CARPENTER. A REALLY GOOD CARPENTER. HE BUILT THE HOUSE WE LIVED IN. I REMEMBER HIM BRINGING THESE PLANKS HOME, SAYING HE WAS FIXING THEM OR REPLACING THEM. NO ONE WOULD HAVE EVER GUESSED DIFFERENTLY. IT WAS HIS JOB TO REPAIR THINGS, AND THEY WERE ALWAYS JUST PLANKS COMING OUT OF THE DREDGE, SO EVEN IF THEY CHECKED, THERE WAS NOTHING TO FIND. AS FAR AS ANYONE ELSE WAS CONCERNED, THE DREDGE WAS SLOWLY GETTING A NEW FLOOR THAT ALWAYS LOOKED BETTER AND BETTER. BUT WHEN THOSE BOARDS WENT BACK, THE CENTERS WERE GONE, READY TO BE FILLED WITH A BLOCK OF PURE GOLD. I GUESS MY OLD MAN WAS PRETTY SMART."

The diagram of the dredge we found in the secret room was very detailed. It showed every floorboard on both floors of the dredge. The ones Joe Bush had filled with gold were colored in with a pencil. There weren't very many empty planks yet to be filled in. In other words, the dredge was a ship of gold. There were hundreds of hidden gold bars.

A year after New York Gold and Silver abandoned dredge #42 in Skeleton Creek, the town bought it for a dollar. There was some talk of turning it into a tourist attraction, but it never materialized. Who wants to walk way out into the woods and look at an old hunk of wood and metal? Nobody, that's who.

But it ended up being the best investment Skeleton Creek ever made.

I got an update from my dad when I came home today. So far they've pulled 1,400 pounds of gold out of the dredge. Every floorboard they pull up has another ten or twenty pounds of pure gold hidden down the middle. The price of gold is high these days, pushing a thousand dollars

AN OUNCE. MY DAD CARRIES A CALCULATOR IN HIS POCKET, ADDING UP THE NUMBERS OVER AND OVER.

"AT A THOUSAND DOLLARS AN OUNCE WE'RE AT SIXTEEN THOUSAND PER POUND OF GOLD," HE TOLD ME EARLIER TODAY. "DO YOU REALIZE HOW MUCH MONEY WHAT THEY'VE FOUND IS WORTH? OVER TWENTY—TWO MILLION BUCKS."

"IT'LL REACH THIRTY MILLION BEFORE THEY'RE DONE TEARING IT APART," I SAID. I'D STUDIED THE DIAGRAM CAREFULLY. THERE WAS A LOT MORE TO BE FOUND.

THIRTY MILLION DOLLARS' WORTH OF GOLD. CAN YOU IMAGINE? AND IT WAS ALWAYS RIGHT THERE, SITTING IN THE WOODS JUST WAITING FOR SOMEONE TO FIND IT.

EVEN THE DREDGE WON'T COME OUT TOO BADLY IN THE END. THERE ARE ALREADY PLANS IN THE WORKS TO BUILD A WOOD—PLANK TRAIL FROM MAIN STREET ALL THE WAY OUT TO THE DREDGE WITH SIGNS ALL ALONG THE WAY DESCRIBING THE AMAZING STORY SARAH AND I UNCOVERED, GHOSTLY SOUNDS AND SITES INCLUDED. THE FACT THAT HENRY HAS GONE MISSING WILL ONLY ADD TO THE URBAN LEGEND AND BRING IN

EVEN MORE TOURISTS. SOME PEOPLE SAY THEY HOPE HE NEVER COMES BACK AND NEVER GETS FOUND.

I AM NOT ONE OF THOSE PEOPLE.

THERE'S TALK OF REBUILDING THE DOWNTOWN AND TURNING SKELETON CREEK INTO A WORLD-CLASS FLY-FISHING AND SIGHTSEEING DESTINATION, WITH THE CREEK AND THE DREDGE AS ITS CENTERPIECE. THIRTY MILLION DOLLARS OUGHT TO COVER IT.

MY DAD'S PLANNING TO OPEN A FLY SHOP, SINCE THE TOWN IS "GIFTING" MY PARENTS AND SARAH'S PARENTS FIVE PERCENT OF WHATEVER COMES OUT OF THE DREDGE.

OH, AND THEY'RE GIVING SARAH AND ME ENOUGH MONEY TO ATTEND ANY COLLEGE WE WANT AFTER GRADUATION. WE'RE CURRENTLY ON THE HUNT FOR A UNIVERSITY KNOWN FOR EXCELLENCE IN BOTH WRITING AND FILMMAKING. I CAN ONLY IMAGINE WHAT KIND OF TROUBLE WE'LL GET INTO WHEN WE SHOW UP ON CAMPUS.

EVERYONE IN SKELETON CREEK SEEMS TO BELIEVE WE CAN TURN THIS PLACE AROUND. STILL, FOR ME, THE TOWN WASN'T THE MOST IMPORTANT THING THE DREDGE GAVE ME BACK.

What I got back, what really matters, is my best friend. They can have all the money as long as they let me and Sarah stay together, which it appears they are going to do. I suppose it would be hard to justify keeping us apart, seeing as how we saved Skeleton Creek and all.

I'm talking to my dad more these days, and he's talking, too. The fly shop will be good for us, a common interest we can share. Plus he'll be around a whole lot more, doing something he loves.

He doesn't talk about Henry. I can't imagine how it would feel for your best friend to betray you like that, to lie about so much for so long. It has softened my dad about me and Sarah, but he's going to have a hard time trusting like that again.

We've both learned a lot about the risks and rewards of friendship.

One of the nice things about being a writer is that writing is always there for me when I need it. During the past few weeks, through all the trauma and loneliness and fear, writing has been

MY REPLACEMENT BEST FRIEND. I'VE SPENT MORE TIME WRITING DURING THE LAST TWENTY DAYS THAN I DID DURING THE HUNDRED DAYS BEFORE THAT. WRITING WAS A COMFORT. I FEEL I OWE IT SOMETHING IN RETURN.

BUT THE PENDULUM IS SWINGING THE OTHER WAY NOW, AND I SUSPECT I'LL BE WRITING A LOT LESS FOR A WHILE. SARAH AND I HAVE SOME CATCHING UP TO DO. THERE'S SCHOOLWORK. I'LL BE DRIVING SOON. I HAVE A STRONG FEELING SARAH WILL WANT TO MAKE A STAB AT LOCATING HENRY, AND I CAN'T LET HER DO IT ALONE.

BUT I KNOW WRITING WILL BE HERE WHEN I NEED IT, AND THIS IS A GREAT COMFORT TO ME AS I VENTURE BACK OUT INTO THE WORLD FULL-TIME.

WE'RE HOSTING A BARBECUE ON THE PORCH TONIGHT, WHICH MEANS I HAVE TO WRAP THIS UP AND GO HELP MY MOM. PRETTY SOON DARYL BONNER AND GLADYS MORGAN WILL BE HERE ALONG WITH A WHOLE BUNCH OF OTHER TOWN FOLKS. SARAH WILL BE HERE WITH HER PARENTS AND HER NEW CAMERA. MY DAD WILL MAN THE GRILL. LATER ON, WHEN THE BUGS START HATCHING AND THE SUN TIPS BEHIND THE MOUNTAINS, I'LL TAKE SARAH TO THE CREEK SO I CAN TEACH HER HOW

TO CAST A FLY ROD. MAYBE WE'LL WALK OUT TO THE DREDGE AND TAKE A LOOK AROUND, OR UP TO LONGHORN'S GRANGE TO RETRIEVE HER DAD'S LADDER OUT OF THE TALL WEEDS.

I CAN'T HELP THINKING ABOUT THAT BLUE ROCK WE PAINTED WHEN WE WERE KIDS AND THE SIMPLE QUESTION SHE ASKED ME.

I WANT TO PAINT THE ROCK, DON'T YOU WANT TO PAINT THE ROCK?

WITHOUT SARAH, I'M NO DIFFERENT THAN THE LEGEND OF OLD JOE BUSH. I'M LIKE A GHOST, ALONE IN MY ROOM, MAKING UP STORIES AND KEEPING TO MYSELF. IT'S LIKE SARAH HAS AHOLD OF MY HAND, PULLING ME FORWARD. SHE'S LOOKING BACK AT ME WITH THE SAME QUESTION IN HER EYES OVER AND OVER AGAIN.

I WANT TO LIVE, DON'T YOU WANT TO LIVE?

I DO, SARAH.

I DO.

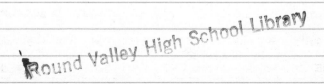

GHOST IN THE MACHINE

PRODUCTION TEAM:

Patrick Carman
Novel/Screenplay

Jeffrey Townsend
Director/Editor/Visual & Audio Effects

Sarah Koenigsberg
Production Manager/Director of Photography

Squire Broel
Production Designer

Amy Vories
Make-Up / Hair / Effects Make-Up

Joseph Ivan Long
Stunt Coordinator

Dave Emigh
Special Props

Amber Larsen
Alternate Camera Operator

Peter Means
Crew

Nick Brandenburg
Crew

Katherine Bairstow
Crew

Joshua Pease
Webmaster / Illustrator

LOCATION ASSISTANCE:

Sumpter Valley Gold Dredge
Oregon Parks and Recreation Department
Miranda Miller, *Park Ranger*
Rella Brown, *Park Host*

Ashley and Brian Rudin

Walla Walla Elks Lodge - Russ Chandler

Sterling Savings Bank - Connie R. Webb, *A.V.P., Branch Manager*

Waitsburg Four Mill - Mayor Markeeta Little

Wolf

Walla Walla Bible Center - Pastor Dave Reed

26brix - George Davis

Merchants Ltd. - Bob Austin

CAST:

Sarah Fincher - Amber Larsen
Ryan McCray - Tom Rowley
Daryl Bonner - Jim Michelson
Paul McCray - Brian Senter
Gladys Morgan - Pat Yenney
Pastor - Ron Davids
The Apostle - Eric Rohde
Dr. Watts - Mark Raddatz

GHOST PERFORMERS

Andrew Latta
Kevin Loomer
Joseph Ivan Long
Ben Boehm
Sarah Koenigsberg
Jeffrey Townsend

MUSIC / SOUNDTRACK

Portfolio Days